This was a

Catherine wa~~s~~
to be. Men lik~~e~~
interested in women like her!

"No," he spoke now, startling her. "I want to go to bed with you. I'd be a fool if I didn't. But not to satisfy some belief that I'm irresistible to women! I'm just a regular guy who finds you very attractive. What's so unusual about that, for heaven's sake?"

Catherine bent her head. "Why?"

"Why what?"

"Why me?" She took an uneven breath. "Did Denzil put you up to it?"

Morgan swore softly, and then, as if unable to prevent himself, he bent toward her, his mouth covering hers....

ANNE MATHER began her career by writing the kind of book she likes to read—romance. Married, with two teenage children, this northern England author has become a favorite with readers of romance fiction the world over—her books have been translated into many languages and are read in countless countries. Since her first novel was published in 1970, Anne Mather has written more than eighty romances, with over ninety million copies sold!

Books by Anne Mather

STORMSPELL
WILD CONCERTO
HIDDEN IN THE FLAME
THE LONGEST PLEASURE

HARLEQUIN PRESENTS
1122—TRIAL OF INNOCENCE
1210—DARK MOSAIC
1251—A FEVER IN THE BLOOD
1315—A RELATIVE BETRAYAL
1354—INDISCRETION
1444—BLIND PASSION

HARLEQUIN ROMANCE
1631—MASQUERADE
1656—AUTUMN OF THE WITCH

ANNE MATHER

such sweet poison

Harlequin Books

TORONTO • NEW YORK • LONDON
AMSTERDAM • PARIS • SYDNEY • HAMBURG
STOCKHOLM • ATHENS • TOKYO • MILAN
MADRID • WARSAW • BUDAPEST • AUCKLAND

Harlequin Presents first edition May 1992
ISBN 0-373-11458-3

Original hardcover edition published in 1991
by Mills & Boon Limited

SUCH SWEET POISON

CHAPTER ONE

'LIVE a little, Cat. He's a friend of Denzil's and he's gorgeous! A little—shy, perhaps, but what the hell? What have you got to lose?'

Catherine Lambert stared at the computer screen in front of her with impatient eyes. 'Since when have Denzil's friends been gorgeous?' she enquired, scowling at the display. 'Damn, that's not right.'

'In this case, he is,' Kay Sawyer assured her swiftly. 'He's an old army buddy of Denzil's. At least, they met while they were both in uniform. Denzil didn't actually see any active service.'

'No.' Catherine allowed a small smile to tilt her lips.

'Well.' Kay was defensive now. 'Denzil's in US Army intelligence, as you know. Someone has to do the boring jobs. We can't all be war heroes, can we?'

Catherine made no comment. Her opinion of Denzil Sawyer was not particularly flattering, but he was Kay's husband, and because of that she was prepared to be tolerant.

'Anyway,' Kay persisted, 'what do you say? You'd be doing me a real favour.'

Catherine looked at the other woman. 'Kay, how many times do I have to tell you? I don't need you to organise my social life.'

'If I don't, you'll spend the next I don't know how many years going home to that empty house, with only that damn moggy for company,' retorted Kay shortly. 'You're a young woman, Cat. Just because—well, just because you made one mistake, you don't have to spend the rest of your life brooding over it.'

5

'I'm not brooding over anything,' Catherine protested, pushing her spectacles up her nose. But it was not precisely true. She always felt a sense of depression whenever she thought about Neil, but she had no intention of admitting that to her friend. 'And Hector's not a moggy,' she added. 'He's a black Persian.'

'All right.' Kay abandoned that tack. 'But how many men have you been out with in the last six months?'

'Does it matter?' A faint trace of colour invaded Catherine's cheeks.

'It matters to me.' Kay sighed. 'Cat——'

'Look, I know you mean well.' Catherine shook her head. 'But honestly, I'd just as soon not get involved.'

'What's involved?' Kay cast her eyes towards the ceiling. 'Cat, this is a dinner invitation, that's all. Nothing more; nothing less.'

Catherine moistened her lips. It was obvious Kay was not going to be put off by prevarication, so she had to think of something else. 'Well, who is he?' she asked. 'What's he doing in England? Is he married?'

Kay glanced quickly round the large office, assuring herself that her conversation was not being observed by a higher authority, and then said confidingly, 'His name's Morgan Lynch, and he's not married.' She shrugged. 'He was—once—but, like you, he's divorced now, and, at present, he's working in Denzil's section at the Embassy.'

'I see.' Catherine bit down on her lower lip. 'Well, I'm sure if you want to ask him to dinner he's quite capable of finding his own date.'

'He doesn't know anybody,' exclaimed Kay frustratedly. 'He's only been in London three weeks! Oh, why can't you just do this one small thing for me?'

Catherine pressed her lips together. 'Does—he—know you're trying to arrange a partner for him?'

'Who? Denzil?' Kay pretended to be obtuse, but when that only aroused a look of resignation she straightened away from Catherine's desk. 'It's only a dinner party,' she said, looking down at her friend with sulky eyes. 'I'm not asking you to go to bed with him. Just to make up a four for a meal.'

Catherine expelled her breath wearily. 'I'd like to help you, Kay, but——'

'But what?'

'Well—as you say—it's been months since I went out— with anyone. Don't you think you ought to ask someone more—sociable?'

Kay shook her head. 'It'll do you good.'

'Will it?' Catherine was not convinced. 'I'm not exactly anyone's idea of a blind date, am I?'

'What do you mean?'

Catherine lifted her shoulders. 'I'm too tall, I'm too fat, and I wear glasses.'

'You're not fat!'

Kay latched on to the only one of the three that was remotely arguable. Catherine was too tall. At five feet ten, she looked down on most of the men she met. Which was one of the reasons Neil had dumped her, Catherine reflected obliquely. He had never liked feeling at a disadvantage, physically or otherwise.

'Anyway, I think you should come,' Kay persisted. 'The trouble with you is, you've had no confidence in yourself since Neil...' She broke off then, as if aware she was invading forbidden territory, and then continued heedlessly, 'Well, it's true. And it's only because I care about you that I say these things. For heaven's sake, it's been almost two years! Don't you think it's about time you made a new start?'

Catherine looped one silky strand of night-dark hair behind her ear. 'By attending your dinner party?' she enquired wryly, and Kay nodded.

'Why not?'

Catherine hesitated. 'Whose idea was it to ask me?' She couldn't believe Denzil Sawyer was in favour. Not after the way she had put him down.

'Denzil's,' declared Kay, astonishingly. 'He said—well, he said you were exactly what—who...' She gave a nervous smile. 'Exactly who we needed.'

Catherine sighed. She suspected there must be something seriously lacking in Morgan Lynch, if Denzil considered her a suitable companion. But she could hardly tell Kay that. Not without getting into a whole nest of sleeping vipers.

The appearance of Kay's boss, Andrew Hollingsworth, one of the senior actuaries, in the office doorway evidently looking for his secretary, made a decision critical. And, although Catherine was sure she was going to regret it later, she decided to accept. After all, Kay was right. Since Neil had walked out on their marriage, she had become virtually a recluse, going from house to office and back again with never a diversion in between.

'All right,' she said, in a low voice, flashing Andrew Hollingsworth a bright smile, and Kay, ever vigilant of any warning signal, gathered up a handful of papers from Catherine's desk, as if that had been her intention all along.

'Do you mean it?' she hissed, as Catherine determinedly rescued the results of the analysis she had been working on, and stared at the now muddled sheets with some frustration.

'Yes. Yes,' she answered, aware that Kay's boss was getting more impatient by the minute. 'Go! I'll talk to you later.'

'Great!' Kay made a circle of her thumb and forefinger, and then, after pulling a face at Catherine, she turned disarmingly towards the door. 'Oh, Mr Hollingsworth! Were you looking for me?'

*   *   *

Of course, Catherine regretted her impulsive decision, as she had known she would. The idea of going to a dinner party—any dinner party—and spending the evening making small talk filled her with dismay. She had never been particularly good at small talk, and, since Neil's defection, she had become increasingly antisocial. Add to that the fact that she knew she had put on weight since the divorce, and that she had nothing suitable to wear, and she had the perfect recipe for depression.

Why ever had she allowed Kay to persuade her? she wondered that evening, as she let herself into her house in Orchard Road. Not even Hector's enthusiastic welcome—rubbing himself about her legs, and emitting little sounds of satisfaction—could lighten her mood. Putting down her briefcase on the hall table, she kicked off her shoes before walking into the kitchen. After all, she thought, opening a cupboard and taking down a tin of tuna, all Hector wanted was feeding. He didn't have any real affection for her. Cats were not like that. Particularly not aristocratic Persians, with more than their fair share of arrogance. He was basically an independent creature; a loner—like herself, she reflected cynically. Only she hadn't been created that way. In her case, it had been a gradual progression.

Hector buried his face in the bowl of fish, and Catherine remained where she was for a moment, gazing out of the window at the garden at the back of the house. Orchard Road was a terrace that had been converted by a developer into a row of modern townhouses, and, in consequence, the garden was very narrow. But it was also quite long, and when she and Neil had first bought the house she had spent hours digging up the weeds, and restoring its former beauty. Someone had once cared about it, and the lawn, and herbaceous border, and the little rockery at the bottom, had all been designed by the previous tenant. Of course now, with the first frosts of winter baring the trees and turning the grass a dirty yellow, it didn't look much as it had looked then. And she didn't have a lot of interest in it these days. Not when she was the only one who was there to appreciate it.

She sometimes wondered whether she would have been wiser to sell this house and buy another. It did hold a lot of painful memories, but after the divorce she hadn't wanted any more changes in her life. Besides, she liked the house, she liked the district, and it was convenient for her job in the City, which meant a lot. Neil hadn't wanted it. He had been quite willing to allow her to buy his half of the house. He and his new wife had an apartment now, in Cavendish Mews. He had moved on from this Fulham backwater. Onwards and upwards, thought Catherine, trying not to feel bitter. But it wasn't always easy.

Leaving Hector to his supper, she walked back along the hall to the stairs. The houses were simply designed: two reception rooms and a kitchen on the ground floor; two bedrooms and a bathroom above. In actual fact, the present kitchen and bathroom owed their existence to the developer. Until the alterations had been made, there had been only two rooms on each floor, with no bathroom, and the only loo at the bottom of the garden.

Thanking whatever providence had decreed that the latter half of the present century should provide basic plumbing amenities for everyone, Catherine went upstairs, walked into the bathroom, and turned on the taps. The bath was another advantage of the house, she reflected, examining the parlour palm which she kept suspended in a wicker planter over the tub. The sunken bath was triangular in shape, and generously proportioned, allowing even Catherine to stretch her long legs.

The main bedroom—*her* bedroom, she was getting used to calling it—was equally attractive. After Neil had left, she had had the functional units he had fitted pulled out, and in their place she had put William Morris wallpaper and walnut furniture. The dressing-table was swagged with a matching fabric, and the enormous quilt, on the newly acquired four-poster, was the same. It was a feminine room, she decided firmly, but not aggressively so. And at least she had a decent job, so that she could afford these little luxuries. If Neil had had his own way, she'd have been completely dependent on him.

Which might have saved their marriage. she reflected now. If she had been prepared to be the little housewife and mother he had wanted, they might still have been together. Of course, the fact that she couldn't have children would have still proved to be a problem. Neil wanted a family. He wanted a son whom he could teach to play golf, and a daughter, to show off to his friends. And when, to add to that, Catherine had obstinately refused to give up her career, the seeds had been sown that had eventually undermined their relationship.

Sliding off her jacket, Catherine unzipped the skirt of her dark grey business suit, and stepped out of it. Then, unbuttoning her blouse, she took that off too, before peeling off her tights. She walked into the bathroom in her camisole and panties, bending to check the heat of the water, before slipping out of her underwear and stepping into the bath. She sank down into the deliciously warm depths with some satisfaction, resting her head back against the tiles and simply enjoying the relaxation.

She did her best thinking in the bath, she thought, the almost embryonic envelopment of the water giving her an unnatural feeling of optimism. At times like these, she could almost convince herself she was happy. She had a comfortable home, a good job, and if she didn't go out a lot that was her fault, not the fault of her friends. There were lots of people far worse off than she was, and she had to stop thinking about the mistakes of the past, and concentrate on the present.

Not least Kay and Denzil's dinner party, she reflected ruefully, reaching for the soap. She still wasn't at all sure how she had been persuaded to accept. Except that Andrew Hollingsworth had been standing in the doorway, and it had seemed politic to bring a swift end to their conversation. But, for heaven's sake, she wasn't afraid of Andrew Hollingsworth. He had no authority over her. Nevertheless, Kay was his secretary, and it was common knowledge that he was becoming increasingly impatient with her propensity to stand gossiping when she had work to do. And if Hollingsworth did fire Kay, she wouldn't find it easy to get another such lucrative position.

And she didn't want that on her conscience, too, Catherine decided, squeezing the soap between her hands and allowing it to plop down into the water. Even if it meant spending another evening in Denzil Sawyer's company. Catherine had never understood what her friend had seen in the brash American diplomat. So far as she was concerned, he was crass, and ill-mannered, and unbearably arrogant when it came to women.

Which was presumably why he and Neil had got along so well, she thought sardonically, searching for the soap again, and beginning to lather her arms. But even Neil would have had a hard time coping with his resentment if he had known that Denzil had had no compunction about making a pass at Catherine, behind his friend's— and his wife's—back. And, what was more, Denzil had initially taken Catherine's rebuttal as a come-on, never admitting the possibility that she might not find him attractive. Of course, when he'd eventually got the message, he had turned nasty. He had used every trick in the book to make Catherine look foolish, but in such a way that, when she complained to Neil, she had appeared prudish. Naturally, she hadn't told Neil the whole truth. Or perhaps not so naturally, she considered now. But she had never really thought that Neil would believe

Denzil might find her more attractive than his vivacious wife, and she hadn't wanted to hurt Kay by breaking up their friendship.

Since the divorce, however, she had had the perfect excuse for refusing their invitations, and that had suited her very well. She and Kay got together for lunch occasionally, but that was all. Catherine had had no intention of exposing herself to Denzil's derision, and it was infuriating to realise she had now done exactly that. But why had he invited her? What was wrong with Morgan Lynch, that Denzil had decided she was the ideal counterpart?

The following evening, Catherine prepared for her dinner engagement without enthusiasm. She didn't feel like going out—but then, she never did. When she got home from the office, she was quite content to bathe and change into baggy pants or a caftan, and spend the evening loafing round the house. She liked to read, and watch television, and sometimes she brought work home with her, and spent the evening at the computer in the spare bedroom, which, since Neil's departure, she had turned into an office.

She knew she ought to go out occasionally. She was living a hermit-like existence, and, for a woman of barely thirty summers, it wasn't healthy. But the trouble was that most of her friends were either married or living with a partner, and she refused to become one of those single women who was every hostess's nightmare. Besides, she had decided she had had enough of men, and marriage. The truth was, she supposed, she still cared about Neil. Even though it was, as Kay had said, two years since their marriage had broken up, she still thought about him, and the love she had thought they shared.

A maudlin thought, decided Catherine now, examining the contents of her wardrobe for something suitable to wear. But, even so, she hadn't expected her first foray into sociability to include spending another evening with the Sawyers. If she had to go out, why couldn't it have been to a restaurant, or to the theatre, with someone fairly anonymous, who didn't know her history? Not this unavoidably intimate gathering, which was bound to spark old memories.

The clothes in the wardrobe were uninspiring, and Catherine sighed. She supposed she should have taken the trouble to go out at lunchtime and buy herself something new and fashionable to wear, but she hadn't felt interested enough to do so. Now, however, she viewed the at-least-two-years-old dresses with a rueful eye, wishing she had something different to wear, if only to avoid their recognition.

The telephone rang as she was riffling through her underwear, and, glad of the diversion, Catherine picked up the phone beside the bed. 'Yes?' she said, trying unsuccessfully to keep the folds of the silk négligé she was wearing around her.

'Catherine? Is that you, darling?'

Recognising her mother's voice, Catherine sighed. 'Who else?' she responded, pulling a face at Hector, who was curled on her bed, licking his paws. Her mother always began her conversations in that way, and Catherine sometimes wondered what she would do if she got a negative answer.

But now she only nodded, and said, 'Yes, Mum. It's me. What can I do for you?'

'Well, you can stop calling me "Mum" for a start,' replied Mrs Lambert staunchly. 'Mother, or Mummy, if you like. But not "Mum"! It's—well, it's not me.'

Catherine made no comment, though she had to admit that her mother did not look like anyone's mum. Mrs Lambert was fifty-two, but she looked years younger, and Catherine occasionally felt like her *older* sister, instead of her only offspring. In her more cynical moments, Catherine had sometimes wondered whether the

fact that Mrs Lambert had been virtually on her own
since Catherine was born had anything to do with it.
Her father, whose job as technical consultant with the
oil industry had taken him all over the world, had been
killed in an explosion in the Middle East when Catherine
was only sixteen, and, since then, her mother had refused to think of marrying anyone else.

Catherine used to think it was because her parents had
been so ideally suited to one another, but now she was
not so sure. Her mother was no one's idea of a grieving
widow. On the contrary, with the salary she earned as
a sales assistant in a rather exclusive gallery, owned by
one of her friends, plus the very generous pension the
oil company paid her, she had become quite a socialite.
And, although she was not short of male admirers, there
was never any question of commitment.

'So,' she went on now, 'how are you? Why haven't I
seen you? Really, Catherine, if it was left to you, we'd
practically be strangers.'

'That's not true.' But Catherine felt a twinge of conscience all the same. It was very infrequently that she
visited her mother's home in Surrey. But the trouble was,
Mrs Lambert showed none of Catherine's own reserve
when it came to arranging Catherine's future for her. In
her opinion, Catherine ought to marry again, if only
because she didn't approve of her job.

'It is true,' Mrs Lambert declared firmly, and
Catherine could tell from the tone of her mother's voice
that she was in for another case of computer bashing.
'And I suppose you're still hibernating every evening.
For heaven's sake, Catherine, you're a young woman.
You should be out every night, having a good time, not
pussy-sitting that precocious tom!'

'Hector's not precocious; he's suspicious of strangers,
that's all,' responded Catherine, choosing the line of least
resistance. 'And he's good company. And undemanding.'

'That's what I mean,' exclaimed her mother impatiently. 'You're getting exactly like your Aunt Agnes. All she's interested in are her cats and her knitting. She won't go anywhere, either, no matter how often I try to be friendly.'

Catherine grimaced. Her father's unmarried sister had always been a thorn in Mrs Lambert's side. There was little to choose between them in age, but a veritable world of difference in attitude. And, although Agnes had done nothing to deserve it, Mrs Lambert had come to the conclusion that she disapproved of her.

'Anyway,' her mother continued, 'I thought, if you weren't doing anything this evening, I might come over. Fliss managed to get a copy of that print you were interested in, so I can bring that with me.'

'No...' Catherine had to stop her before she talked herself into ringing off. Even though she had hoped to avoid telling her mother what she was doing that evening, and the inevitable questions it would arouse, there was no help for it. She had to admit she was going out.

'No?' Mrs Lambert interrupted her train of thought. 'Why not?'

Catherine sighed. 'Well—as a matter of fact, I'm going out to dinner.'

'You are?' There was a wealth of expression in her mother's voice. 'Who with? Not that nice young man from the office.'

The nice young man from the office her mother was referring to was Simon Lewis, one of Catherine's fellow analysts. In a weak moment, she had once mentioned that he had asked her out, and since then Mrs Lambert regularly brought his name into the conversation. The fact that Catherine wasn't interested in him made no significant difference to her mother's attitude. So far as Mrs Lambert was concerned, he was unmarried, therefore he was eligible. Catherine sometimes wondered what her mother would say if she asked her why she didn't practise what she preached.

Now, however, though it was tempting to allow Mrs Lambert to think she was having dinner with Simon, Catherine had to be honest. Besides, it would probably be simpler in the long run. The last thing she wanted was to give her mother any grounds for thinking she was starting a relationship.

'Actually, I'm having dinner with Kay and Denzil,' she admitted reluctantly. 'Sorry.'

'Kay and Denzil Sawyer?' The enthusiasm had died out of her mother's voice. 'Whatever for? I thought you didn't like Kay's husband.'

'I don't.' Catherine cast her eyes towards the ceiling. Then, dragging her négligé about her, she flopped down on to the bed, causing Hector to utter a wounded miaow before beating a less than dignified retreat. 'Mum—*my*, they're not *taking me* anywhere. We're having dinner at home.'

'Just the three of you?'

Mrs Lambert was horribly tenacious, and Catherine wondered how she would like it if she put her mother through this kind of catechism before she spent the evening with friends—well, *one* friend, at least.

Deciding there was nothing for it but to be completely frank, she said flatly, 'No, not just the three of us. A friend of Denzil's will be there as well.'

'A friend? You mean another man.'

'An old army buddy, apparently,' agreed Catherine, gradually losing patience. 'And I'm not even ready yet, so unless you've something important to tell me, can we wind this up?'

'Well, who is he?'

The interest was back, and Catherine wanted to scream. 'I don't know,' she lied, not prepared to go any further with this. 'And don't start imagining there's anything more to it than that. End of story.'

Her mother snorted. 'I wouldn't have thought you were any friend of Denzil Sawyer's type,' she remarked tartly, unconsciously echoing Catherine's own suspicions. 'Oh well...' She made a sound of resignation. 'I suppose you know what you're doing.'

'I'm only going out for dinner.' Catherine knew she sounded defensive now, and it was infuriating. 'I'll speak to you later, right? Um—thanks for getting the print. I'll come down and get it this weekend, if that's all right with you.'

'I suppose so.'

There was a trace of coolness in Mrs Lambert's voice now, and Catherine uttered a rude word as she put down the phone. Honestly, she thought, giving her reflection a baleful look, it was just her luck that her mother had to choose tonight, of all nights, to ring. As if she didn't have enough to worry about, what with not knowing what to wear, and anticipating the evening ahead with about as much enthusiasm as she would have had for her own execution. Her mother's disapproval was all she needed to make her wish she had stuck to her original intentions.

Still, half an hour later, she was ready—as she would ever be, she appended, viewing her reflection in the long mirrors of the wardrobe. The black silk jersey was not new, but at least its lines were simple and unpretentious. And the cowl neckline did flatter the slender column of her neck, she thought, pulling the silky straight hair out of her collar. It was just a pity her hair was so dark. She would have to add a brooch, or, with her sallow skin, she would look as if she were going to a funeral.

The short skirt was probably an advantage, she decided. Her legs were undoubtedly her best feature. Unlike the rather too generous breasts concealed by the loosely draped bodice. She really would have to consider a diet. But, living alone, it never seemed to have any purpose.

Behind their tortoiseshell frames, however, her grey eyes took in her appearance with undisguised cynicism. Did it really matter what she looked like? she wondered. So far as Denzil Sawyer was concerned, she would always be a source of aggravation, and the butt of his unkind humour. He had never forgiven her for turning him down, and in spite of this invitation she had no reason to believe he felt any differently now.

Hector voiced his protest that she was leaving him alone for the evening as she put on her cream cashmere overcoat. Twining himself around her legs, he did his best to prevent her from walking towards the door, and she bent to scratch his ears before picking up her gloves.

'Sorry,' she said sympathetically, pulling a face. 'Believe me, this wasn't my idea.'

CHAPTER TWO

CATHERINE'S small Peugeot was housed at the end of the street. A row of garages had been built to accommodate the needs of the townhouse owners, and, while it wasn't as convenient as having a garage next to the house, it was better than nothing. Besides, Catherine only used her car if she went out in the evening, or at weekends. During the day, it was easier to use public transport to get to work.

The Sawyers lived in St John's Wood. Their house was a tall, narrow Victorian dwelling, with no garden to speak of, and three shallow steps leading up to the front door. It was in one of those busy roads where there was seldom anywhere to park, but Catherine managed to squeeze the Peugeot between a Volvo and a Rolls-Royce. She climbed out reluctantly, hoping it would still be there when she got back. Her mother was always telling her she should have an alarm fitted, but somehow she never got round to it. Much like everything else, except her work, she mused, locking the car. So what was she doing here?

Kay herself answered the door to her ring, and her attractive features broke into a relieved smile at the sight of her friend. 'We were beginning to think you must have had an accident,' she exclaimed, inviting Catherine into the discreetly lit hallway of the house. 'Here—let me take your coat. Mrs Chivers is busy with the dinner.'

Catherine slipped off the cashmere overcoat, shifting her bag and gloves from one hand to the other as she did so. Since she had last been here, the hall had been decorated, and she tried to divert her mind from the evening ahead by admiring the plaster dado, and the elegantly striped paper above.

'Oh, a friend of Denzil's did it,' said Kay carelessly, when Catherine complimented her on the improvement. And then, evidently more concerned about her friend's late arrival than their decorations, she added, 'What happened? Couldn't you get parked? You should have taken a taxi.'

Catherine checked she was still wearing both of the convex squares of gold she had clipped to her ears, and suppressed a faint sigh. 'I—my mother rang,' she explained, letting Kay take her gloves and lay them on the hall table. She checked her watch. 'Am I so late?'

Kay expelled her breath heavily. 'Oh—not especially, I suppose,' she conceded. 'But we are eating at eight, and it's a quarter to now.'

Catherine grimaced. 'I'm sorry.'

'That's all right,' Kay seemed to realise she was being ungracious, and gave a rueful smile. 'So—come on. Denzil and Morgan are in the drawing-room.'

Catherine followed her friend up the stairs, wondering how soon after dinner she could make her escape. Not immediately, perhaps, but after coffee...

'Here she is.'

Kay led the way into the first floor drawing-room, and her announcement made Catherine feel even worse. She felt as if she were attending an interview, and she had kept her would-be employers waiting. Belatedly, she realised that she should have got there before Morgan Lynch. Then she would have had the advantage, and not the other way about.

The drawing-room was high-ceilinged and spacious, a clever amalgamation of two of the house's previous rooms into an imposing, and elegant, living area. And, in keeping with the period of the house, the Sawyers had bought some of the more attractive items of Victorian furniture, which blended well with a modern desire for comfort.

As Catherine followed Kay into the room, two men rose from the high-backed wing chairs that flanked the marble fireplace. A convincing blaze burned in the grate, and had Catherine not known better she would have sworn the fire was real. But it wasn't. It was only a gas facsimile, its flickering flames dispersing the shadows, and lighting the dark planes in the face of the man she assumed was Morgan Lynch.

Her balance tipped for a moment as she met his guarded gaze. In spite of what Kay had said, she had not expected to find him at all attractive, and it was a little unnerving to find how wrong she had been. She noticed the way he moved first, the lithe, easy way he pushed himself up out of the chair. Although he was tall—easily six feet two or three—his height was not a problem to him. He was wearing a suit, a three-piece suit of fine dark wool, which fitted the supple contours of his body with a loving attention to detail, casually outlining the width of his shoulders, and more subtly defining his hips. He was lean, possibly too lean when compared to Denzil's more generous proportions, but it was not a distraction. And his legs were long and powerful, the muscles moving fluidly beneath the tautly draped fabric.

But, although she took in these extraneous details, it was his face her eyes were drawn to: the deeply set eyes, beneath hooded brows, whose colour was indefinable, within their veil of long dark lashes; the high cheek-bones, and straight nose; the hollows in his cheeks; and his mouth, with its fuller lower lip—an undoubted trace of sensuality. His hair was dark—not as dark as hers perhaps, but a rich dark brown. It was thick and straight, and lay close to his head. It was just a little too long at the back, and overlapped his collar slightly, but it all added to his appeal. Without doubt, he was one of the most attractive men she had ever seen, and she sensed Kay and Denzil watching her, gauging her reaction.

'Cat—darling!' Denzil's greeting was unusually fulsome, and he came to take her hand between both of his, before bestowing an unwelcome kiss on her cheek. 'You look—wonderful,' he added, the slight hesitation before the compliment not lost on its recipient. 'Come and meet an old friend of mine from the old days, Morgan Lynch. Morgan, this is Catherine—Cat!' He gave a smug smile. 'But don't worry, old buddy, I've pulled her claws, haven't I, Cat?'

Fortunately Catherine was able to ignore Denzil's sarcasm. Morgan Lynch was shaking her hand, and his polite, 'Hello, Catherine,' completely obliterated the other man's innuendo. His voice was low and deep, with a decided Southern drawl, but, although his words were friendly, his attitude was strangely withdrawn.

He was evidently nothing like Denzil, thought Catherine, as he drew back to allow Kay into their circle. He had none of the brash presumption of his own importance that Denzil exhibited at every turn. Kay had said he was shy, and Catherine had to believe her. What other reason could he have for standing silently by while his host and hostess struggled to include him?

Was that why Kay had been so touchy when she arrived? Catherine wondered. It was not like her friend to pay such strict attention to the time. She couldn't ever remember Kay being in such a state before. But what made them think she would have any more success?

'So—what can I get you to drink, Cat?' Denzil enquired now, indicating the tray of drinks on the bookcase behind him. 'I think we've got everything. Well, I know I have,' he added suggestively, thumping Morgan on the back. 'How about you, old buddy?'

Morgan flinched. There was no other way to describe his reaction to Denzil's back-slapping joviality, and both Kay and Denzil looked uncomfortable now. There was another awkward silence, during which Kay exchanged a killing look with her husband, before Catherine recovered sufficiently to say, 'Just bitter lemon, please. I—er—I'm driving.'

'You should have taken a taxi,' said Kay, obviously so grateful for the diversion that she didn't realise she was repeating what she had said downstairs. 'You have to be so careful nowadays, don't you, Denzil?'

'What? Oh, yes.' Denzil turned from pouring Catherine's drink and handed her the glass. He looked awkwardly at Morgan. 'A refill, old man?'

'No, thanks.'

Morgan covered the glass he was holding in his left hand with his right, and seeing the unbecoming rise of colour in Denzil's cheeks, Catherine got a notion as to why she had been invited this evening. Morgan's line in small talk was even less accomplished than her own, and she could understand Denzil not wanting to involve anyone who mattered to him.

'Oh, well, we'll be eating soon,' Kay murmured, giving Catherine a rueful smile. 'I hope you like asparagus. I found this really unusual recipe for a cream cheese and asparagus mousse.'

'It sounds delicious,' said Catherine, cradling her glass between her palms. 'Did you make it or Mrs Chivers?'

'Mrs Chivers, I'm afraid.' Kay grimaced. 'Cooking's not my strong point, as you should know. Do you still make that luscious goulash, you used to make when—when...'

Her voice tailed off as she realised where the conversation was taking her, and Catherine, aware of what she had been about to say, made an effort to relieve the situation.

'Not often,' she said, taking a sip of her bitter lemon, and allowing her eyes to move to each of them in turn, safe behind the screen of the glass. 'I'm afraid I've become rather lazy. There's not much fun in cooking for one.'

'Catherine lives alone,' put in Denzil, as if that particular observation was necessary. His eyes flickered broodingly over his wife's friend. 'I must say, Cat, you don't look as if you've been starving yourself.'

'Nor do you,' retorted Catherine tartly, and Denzil automatically sucked in his belly, which protruded over the waistband of his trousers. She turned to Morgan. 'Do you cook for yourself, er—Morgan?'

'Occasionally.' Morgan inclined his head towards her. 'But, like you, I live alone. Food doesn't come too high on my list of priorities.'

Catherine noticed that both Kay and Denzil looked vaguely startled at this, and she guessed it was the longest statement Morgan had uttered since he came into the house. But why had Denzil invited him, if he was so excessively uncommunicative?

'I bet I can guess what does come high on your list of priorities, old buddy,' Denzil insinuated slyly, and Catherine wondered how he could be so crass. It was obvious that his kind of humour was not appreciated by either of his guests, yet he persisted in making these asinine remarks.

'I doubt it,' Morgan replied, regarding him in a way that would have made a more sensitive man shrivel, and Kay, sensing a possible confrontation, rushed in with a comment about the weather. It was becoming increasingly obvious that whatever Denzil and Morgan were to one another, it was not friends, and Catherine was convinced now that that was why she was here tonight.

Mrs Chivers's appearance to announce that the meal was ready came as an enormous relief to all of them. Well, to three of them it did, Catherine amended drily. She was not at all certain how Morgan felt. It was impossible to judge what he was feeling behind that guarded façade, and his brief spurt of confidence was not repeated, as they were served the delicious asparagus mousse, rack of lamb with new potatoes, peas, and carrots, then a flaming baked Alaska.

During the meal, Catherine made an effort to talk to Kay at least, and their inconsequential chatter made it appear that they were enjoying themselves. But when the talk moved to Kay's job, and her regular disagreements with Andrew Hollingsworth, Morgan looked at Catherine over the rim of his wine glass.

'Are you a secretary, too, Catherine?' he enquired, arching one dark eyebrow, and, although it was ridiculous, she could feel the colour invading her cheeks at his unexpected involvement.

'Er—no——' she was beginning awkwardly, when Kay interceded on her behalf.

'Nothing so commonplace,' she said, and her smile was only slightly waspish. 'Cat's an investment analyst. She tells my boss how to spend his money.'

'Hardly that,' murmured Catherine, giving her friend a dry look, and Denzil chose that moment to make his contribution.

'Cat's a career woman,' he said, pouring himself more wine. 'A real workaholic. She's not interested in men, are you, Cat? Except as figures on a balance sheet, of course.'

Catherine never knew how she stopped herself from telling Denzil Sawyer exactly what she thought of his petty efforts to embarrass her. She knew it was another attempt to get back at her for turning him down, and she wished she had the nerve to expose his real character.

But she couldn't do that. Not to Kay. So, after a moment, she said, 'If it makes you happy to think that, why not?' choosing the line of defence which she knew would infuriate him. She pushed her spectacles up her nose in a decidedly defiant gesture. 'I think Denzil finds independent women threatening,' she added, to the table in general. She adopted a sympathetic smile. 'Poor

Denzil. He tries so hard to be progressive. It's a pity he doesn't succeed.'

Denzil's face was a picture, but, short of being downright rude, there was little he could say. 'Well, thank heavens, Kay only works because it suits her,' he declared, through tight lips. 'Not because it's the only successful aspect of her life!'

'Denzil!'

Kay was embarrassed now, and, as Catherine was searching for a response which would not reveal how Denzil's words had stung her, Morgan chose to intervene.

'What does an investment analyst do?' he enquired, ignoring Kay's abortive attempts to silence her husband. 'I guess it has something to do with the stock market.'

'Well, there's a lot of bull involved, if that's what you mean,' Denzil retorted, riding high on his previous success. 'Bulls, and bears, and a few cows thrown in, for good measure, eh, Cat?'

'Why don't you just shut your fat mouth?'

Morgan's tone was almost silkily pleasant, but his words were clear and unmistakable. Both Kay and Denzil gasped at the unexpectedness of his attack, and even Catherine was astounded by his insolence.

'Now, look here...' Shaking off his wife's warning hand, Denzil's face contorted. 'You can't talk to me like that,' he snarled, getting to his feet and looking down at the other man.

'Can't I?'

Matching Denzil's move, Morgan pushed back his chair and stood up, his superior height automatically signalling a change of status. He rested the tips of his fingers on the table, and regarded the other man steadily. His features were completely expressionless and curiously lacking in emotion.

'No, you can't,' muttered Denzil, less convincingly. He met Morgan's eyes, and then looked away, encountering his wife's anxious gaze in the process. 'For God's

sake, man, can't you take a joke?' he mumbled, his
whole aggressive demeanour crumbling. 'Cat wasn't offended, were you, Cat? She knows I don't mean any
harm. Isn't that right?'

He was appealing to her now, and, while Catherine
would have liked to savour such a moment, she knew it
was up to her to rescue the situation. For Kay's sake, if
nothing else.

'Please,' she said, not prepared to accept Denzil's
grudging apology, but looking up at Morgan with rueful
eyes, 'won't you sit down again? Denzil's tongue often
runs ahead of his brains. I'm used to it.'

It wasn't what Denzil wanted to hear, she knew, and
his sulky expression boded ill for her friendship with
Kay. But at least Morgan seemed prepared to accept her
explanation, and, although he waited until Denzil had
resumed his seat before sinking back into his chair, the
crisis was averted.

However, there was little chance for normal conversation after that, and, although Catherine made an effort
to talk to Kay, she was glad when the coffee was served,
and she could think about leaving. What a dinner party!
she thought, keeping her eyes firmly fixed on the coffee
in her cup. So what if it misted her spectacles? Better
that than meeting Denzil's malevolent stare.

'Well,' she said, when Mrs Chivers came to ask if
anyone wanted any more coffee, 'I think I ought to be
going.'

'Oh, no.' Kay's protest was genuine, Catherine was
sure, but she couldn't be expected to act as a buffer between the two men any longer.

'I'm sorry,' she said, giving Kay a wry smile. 'But I
do have to be in early tomorrow. Besides, Hector isn't
used to spending the whole evening on his own. And,
as Denzil says, you do have to keep your priorities in
order.'

Kay sighed. 'Well—if you must . . .'

'Perhaps I can give you a ride home,' said Morgan abruptly, and Catherine turned to look at him with startled eyes. 'I just need to phone my driver. If you can hang on for fifteen minutes——'

'I have my own transport, actually.' Catherine interrupted him, with a nervous gesture of her hand. 'But, thank you, all the same...'

'Why don't you give Morgan a lift?' Kay suggested, the swiftness of her question revealing the urgency with which she wished they would both leave. She flushed a little as Catherine turned to stare at her. 'Well,' she murmured, defensively, 'it's not much out of your way.'

'That won't be necessary,' Morgan interposed, getting up from the table with the litheness of movement Catherine was beginning to associate with him. 'As a matter of fact, I think I'll walk. I could use the exercise.'

Now Catherine felt mean. 'Don't be silly,' she said, exchanging a frustrated look with Kay, as she got to her feet, too. 'Of course, I'd be happy to give you a lift. Where exactly do you live?'

'It doesn't matter——'

'Bayswater.'

Both Morgan and Kay spoke simultaneously, but it was Morgan who had the last word.

'I'd prefer to walk,' he averred, drawing Catherine's chair away from the back of her legs, so that she could move towards the door. He looked at Denzil. 'Goodnight.'

''Night.'

Denzil didn't get up, and Catherine guessed it was his way of showing his defiance. But it was a childish defiance at best, and she thought Kay looked at him a little disgustedly as she led the way downstairs.

Kay rescued her cashmere coat from the hall closet, but Morgan apparently had no overcoat. Not that he seemed at all perturbed. Even when the door was opened, and it was discovered to be raining, he showed no

concern. He merely thanked Kay for dinner, and offered
them both a polite 'Goodnight', before striding off into
the darkness. Catherine was left to bid farewell to her
friend, in the certain knowledge that nothing between
them would ever be the same.

'I'll see you tomorrow, then,' Kay offered, as
Catherine stepped out of the door.

'Yes,' Catherine cast a rueful look up at the rain,
clearly visible in the streetlights. 'What a filthy night!'

'Yes, isn't it?' Kay grimaced, and then added swiftly,
'I'm sorry, Cat. I didn't know...' She shrugged, and
glanced back over her shoulder. 'You know.'

Catherine shook her head. 'Forget it.'

'I can't.' Kay bit her lip. 'But you know Denzil, don't
you? He doesn't mean what he says. It's just the wine
talking, that's all.'

'Hmm.' Catherine nodded. 'Well—thanks for dinner,
anyway.'

'Don't thank me. You hardly ate anything,' exclaimed
Kay unhappily.

'Well, what I did eat was good,' Catherine assured
her, going down the steps. 'See you in the morning.'

'Yes. We'll talk then,' Kay agreed eagerly, and, the
way her eyes darted up the road after Morgan's de-
parting figure, Catherine could guess what she wanted
to talk about. 'Goodnight.'

'Goodnight.'

Catherine lifted her hand in farewell, and, turning up
her collar against the rain, she started across the road
to her car. She was glad Kay closed the door behind her,
and didn't wait to see her extract the Peugeot from between its two bulky neighbours. It would have been hyp-
ocritical to behave as if it had been a perfectly normal
evening, when it so obviously hadn't.

She would have liked to have driven away in the opposite direction to that which Morgan had taken, but
her car was pointing the same way, and it was going to

be too much trouble to turn it around. Besides, why should she go miles out of her way, just to avoid passing him? she thought defensively. She had nothing to be ashamed of. She had offered him a lift, and he had refused. That was all there was to it. If he chose to walk home on a cold, wet October evening, it wasn't her concern.

Even so, she wasn't happy about it. He had apparently been driven to the Sawyers' in a chauffeured car, and he had obviously been expected to go home likewise. She didn't know why he should have warranted a car and a driver. To her knowledge, Denzil had never been granted that privilege. But perhaps they had simply been hired for the evening, from an agency. Whatever, it was foolish to consider walking any distance tonight. With colds and flu to contend with, a person was asking for trouble going out in the rain, without an overcoat.

As she eased the Peugeot out from the kerb, she thought about the fine wool suit he had been wearing— the suit, which had fitted his lean body so immaculately. It wouldn't look so immaculate now, she thought impatiently. In this downpour, it would soon resemble a wet rag.

The Peugeot picked up speed as she moved out into the traffic. She raised her hand in thanks to the driver behind her, who had flashed his headlights to signal her to come out, but her eyes were already searching for a tall, dark pedestrian. It was stupid really, but she felt responsible. If she hadn't been so churlish over offering him a lift, the idea of walking would probably not have occurred to him.

She hadn't gone far when she saw him. Even though he had left the Sawyers' at a brisk rate, his pace had slowed considerably. Indeed, with his hands pushed into the pockets of his jacket, he might have been taking a summer evening's stroll. People he was passing, wrapped up in coats and scarves, and carrying umbrellas, turned

to stare at him in amazement. They probably thought
he was crazy, thought Catherine, gritting her teeth.
Possibly he was.

Even so, she couldn't pass him by. Ignoring the noisy
protest from the driver who, minutes before, had so
courteously let her out into the stream of traffic, she
braked hard, and pulled over to the kerb. She was in an
area where there were several small boutiques and a
Chinese restaurant and, aware that she was parking in
a no-parking area, she didn't waste any time.

'Get in,' she yelled, leaning across the passenger seat,
and pushing open the door. 'You can't walk to Bayswater
in this. Come on. I'll take you.'

At first, she thought he was going to refuse. Although
he stopped, and looked in her direction, he made no
move to get into the little car, and Catherine wanted to
scream. However, the cacophony of horns blowing
behind her, which drew attention to the fact that she was
causing a hold-up, seemed to galvanise him into action.
Without saying a word, he crossed the pavement, and
folded his long length into the seat beside her, closing
the door behind him with a carefully controlled click.

'Seatbelt,' said Catherine automatically, pressing her
foot down hard on the accelerator, and, although he gave
her what she could only describe as an unfriendly look,
he did as he was told. Nevertheless, he made no attempt
to speak to her, and the atmosphere in the car went from
cordial to hostile in the space of a few seconds.

The whole ambience of the car had changed, thought
Catherine irritably, half wishing she had not been so impulsive. Where before there had been only the fragrance
of her own perfume to invade her nostrils, now all she
could smell was the musky odour of wet wool, and the
masculine scent of his body.

Pushing up her spectacles again, as she was inclined
to do in situations of stress, she said shortly, 'Where

exactly do you live? I don't know Bayswater awfully well, so you'll have to direct me.'

Morgan turned his head and looked at her before replying. Then, loosening the button of his shirt beneath his tie, and pulling the tie a few inches away from his neck, he said flatly, 'I don't know Bayswater either.'

Catherine cast a disbelieving glance in his direction. In the light from the street lamps outside, she could see that his hair was soaked and dripping down the opened neck of his shirt. His jacket was soaked, too, and she guessed from its appearance that he was probably wet right through to his skin.

To her annoyance, it gave her a disturbing feeling thinking of Morgan's skin, and, to hide her disconcertment, she said, more sharply than she would have done, 'Don't be silly! You have to know your address.'

'Do I?' He lifted his shoulders, and she heard the damp sibilation of the cloth against the upholstery.

'Of course.' She sighed. 'Look, you're soaked to the skin. The sooner you get out of those wet clothes, the better.'

'I agree.'

Morgan inclined his head, and to her astonishment, he tugged off his tie and dropped it on to the floor. His jacket followed, and the satin-lined waistcoat, a couple of the buttons on his shirt pinging against the car windows as he yanked it open to join the rest.

'Hey—stop it!'

Catherine was horrified now, her hands trembling as they gripped the wheel. She couldn't believe anyone would do such a thing, and her startled glance took in the silhouette of his leanly muscled chest with some disbelief. He couldn't be doing this, she told herself fiercely, but already his hands were moving to the belt that held up his trousers, and she couldn't pretend it wasn't happening.

'What's wrong?' he asked, giving her a sidelong glance. 'I thought you said the sooner I got out of these wet clothes, the better.'

'You knew what I meant by that,' retorted Catherine tensely. 'Please—people can see you!'

'Can they?' He cast his eyes towards the misted windows. 'I doubt it. But even if they can, so what?'

Catherine gasped. 'Are you mad?'

'I guess.'

It was not the answer she had expected, and Catherine almost ran into the car in front of her as she turned wide eyes in his direction. 'Don't joke about things like that,' she exclaimed, when she had recovered from the shock of almost causing an accident.

'Who's joking?' he responded, and she saw the convulsive shudder that ran over him as the still-cool air in the car attacked his naked flesh.

Catherine shook her head, trying to concentrate on the road ahead. But she didn't know what to do, what to say. In retrospect, the rest of the evening seemed like a sinecure compared to this. What was he trying to prove?

'1805, Jermyn Gate,' said Morgan abruptly, dragging the sleeves of his shirt out of the sleeves of his waistcoat, and putting the shirt back on.

'I beg your pardon?'

Catherine had been so wrapped up with her own thoughts that she didn't immediately comprehend what he was saying, and Morgan regarded her quizzically for a moment, before saying again, '1805, Jermyn Gate. That's my address.'

Catherine blinked behind her spectacles. 'Well—where's that?'

'Your guess is as good as mine,' declared her passenger, shivering again as the damp silk of his shirt touched his flesh. 'Somewhere off the Bayswater Road. I guess I could find it in daylight, but tonight...' He shrugged expressively. 'Just drop me here. I'll pick up a cab.'

Here was at the junction of St John's Wood Road and Edgware Road, but, although there were plenty of people, as well as traffic, about, Catherine didn't stop the car. She couldn't put him out here, she thought, imagining what a taxi driver would think if he saw a man in his shirt sleeves, in the pouring rain, thumbing a ride. Heavens, he could get arrested! She knew he hadn't drunk much during the course of the evening, but would anyone else believe it?

Coming to what she hoped would not prove to be a reckless decision, Catherine shook her head, abandoning that idea, and took the next turning for Kensington. It would be easier to use the bypass, she thought, mentally calculating the advantages of staying out of central London. She could double back to Shepherd's Bush when she reached Wood Lane.

'It depends where you're going, I suppose,' she said, her hands tightening on the wheel. 'You can't get a taxi in that state.'

Morgan's dark brows drew together. 'So where are we going? To your place?'

'Only to dry your clothes,' retorted Catherine shortly, not liking the cynical note in his voice. 'I'm not interested in you, Mr Lynch, if that's what you're thinking.'

'Only in cementing East-West relations, right?' he remarked, his eyes sardonically intent. 'What about this guy—Hector, didn't you say? Won't he object to an unwelcome visitor?'

Catherine caught her breath. She wouldn't have expected him to remember what she had said to Kay. 'Er—Hector's my cat,' she admitted, glad that the visibility in the car did not extend to colour. 'As your— friend was at pains to tell you, I live alone.'

Morgan's eyes darkened. 'OK. If that's what you want.'

'It's not what *I* want,' said Catherine brusquely. 'I'd have preferred you to call your driver from the Sawyers', and have him take you home, as any sane person would have done on a night like tonight!'

'So why are you doing this?' Morgan's voice was harsh now. He put one hand on the steering-wheel, and she was terrified for a moment that he was going to turn the car into the oncoming traffic. 'Aren't you afraid I might prove to be a psycho? I mean, you said yourself that you have doubts about my sanity.'

'I didn't say that.' Catherine's knuckles were white around the leather grip. 'I just meant it wasn't...sensible...to walk home on a night like this. You could—take a chill. Pneumonia!'

Morgan released the wheel, and his hand dropped on to his thigh. 'Your speech sure is littered with pretty words,' he declared caustically. 'I guess that's why old Denny was busting a gut to please you!'

Old Denny? For a moment, Catherine couldn't think who he was talking about. But then, the penny dropped. Denny—*Denzil*! Strangely enough, the abbreviation pleased her. She could imagine how Denzil would react to such a disparaging appellation.

'He said—that is, *Kay* said—you and he were old friends,' she ventured. 'But you're not. You—don't like him, do you?'

Morgan shrugged. 'Do you?'

'No.' Catherine moistened her lips. 'But I asked you the question first.'

Morgan sighed. 'Denny and I go way back,' he said, without elaborating. Then, glancing out of the window, 'How much further is this apartment of yours?'

Catherine hesitated. 'It's not an apartment. It's a house. Just a small one. And—it's not much further. About half a mile, that's all.'

'Good.'

Morgan ran his hand along his damp thigh, and, although she didn't want to, Catherine couldn't help observing the action. His long fingers stretched the cloth over the relaxed, yet powerful muscles of his leg, and she felt an unwelcome awareness assault her senses. It was because it was so long since she had been alone with a man, she told herself severely, but it wasn't entirely the truth. His sexuality disturbed her as no man's ever had—not even Neil's.

She decided not to park the car in the garage. It would be easier to park outside her gate, and run the half-dozen yards to her door. Besides, the last thing she wanted was for any of her neighbours to see her coming home with a man who looked as if he'd just got out of bed.

'This it?' enquired Morgan, as she drew the car to a halt, and Catherine nodded. Now that they were actually here, she was beginning to realise how reckless she had been. What did she know about this man, after all? Except that he was crazy enough to attempt a strip in her car. The excitement he engendered in her was no excuse for inviting him to her home. Quite the opposite, in fact.

Still, it was a little late now to be having second thoughts, she reflected wryly. They were here, and she was committed to drying his clothes and calling him a taxi, at the very least. On top of which, she was flattering herself if she imagined he had any interest in her. She had brought him here. He had had nothing to do with it.

Pulling the keys out of the ignition, she pushed open her door. Morgan did likewise, standing for a moment in the road, looking up at the narrow frontage of the house. It was still raining, but he didn't seem to notice how wet it was. Slicking back his soaking hair with a lazy hand, he sauntered round the car, while Catherine fled up the path to the door, in a hasty rush for shelter.

'Come on,' she said, turning on the hall light, and hovering on the threshold. 'Can't you hurry? You're getting even wetter.'

'You can't get wetter than wet,' retorted Morgan, in a careless drawl, stepping after her into the hall, and instantly dwarfing it. 'Don't worry about it. I've been wet before.'

Catherine shook her head as he leaned his shoulders against the door, and pressed it closed behind him. The Yale lock dropped into place, securing her inside, with him, and for the first time she regretted that Hector wasn't a Dobermann. Protective as he was, Hector was nobody's idea of a bodyguard.

But, as if the thought was father to the deed, Hector chose that moment to come stalking out of the living-room. He had evidently heard the strange voice, and, with his head held high, and his long fur bristling, he did look aggressive. But although he emitted a few protesting miaows, he confined his resistance to arching his tail.

'I guess this is Hector, hmm?' Morgan remarked humorously, dropping his jacket over the banister rail, and squatting down beside him. 'Hey, there, fella, aren't you some dude! You want to be friends?'

Hector's growl was reassuring, and he backed away behind Catherine's legs, evidently not prepared to be sociable. Indeed, as she bent to pick him up, Catherine could feel his little heart pounding away, and she felt a sense of pride in his loyalty.

Morgan straightened. 'Suspicious little beast, isn't he?' he observed, without rancour. 'What is he? A Persian?'

'Yes.' Catherine was surprised that he knew. She rubbed her cheek against Hector's fine hair for a moment, and then deposited him in the sitting-room again, and closed the door. 'I've had him for the last two years, and he's not used to strangers.'

'No.' Morgan inclined his head, his wet hair flopping over his forehead. 'Cats are very territorial. They don't like other males invading their domain.'

Catherine's lips tightened. 'You're hardly an invader,' she declared, lifting his wet jacket off the banister, and grimacing as some drops of water fell on to her feet.

'He doesn't know that,' replied Morgan, his smile faintly mocking. 'So—where do I change my clothes? Would you like me to do it here?'

'In the hall! Of course not.' Catherine hesitated a moment, and then, walking quickly along the hall to the kitchen, she dropped the offending jacket on to the stripped pine table.

However, when she turned round, he was right behind her, and her breath caught in her throat as she rammed into his chest. He sucked in his breath, too, and she thought for a moment that a spasm of pain crossed his face. But then he recovered himself swiftly, and stepped back, allowing Catherine the space to move around him.

'We—we might as well go upstairs,' she said, brushing past him, supremely conscious of how hard and un-yielding his muscled stomach had felt beneath her hands. The thin shirt was hardly a barrier to his taut flesh, but its clammy feel was a sharp reminder of how cold he must be.

'OK.'

After a brief glance at his jacket, Morgan followed her back along the hall and up the stairs. From the sitting-room, Catherine could hear Hector's protesting wail, but she determinedly ignored it. Whatever happened, he was not going to be of much use, and he might prove more of a hindrance under her feet. Her bedroom had never looked more feminine than when Morgan halted in the doorway, supporting himself against the whitewood frame. Although she had been married to Neil for almost five years, at that moment she felt decidedly spinsterish. And Morgan probably knew it, she thought impatiently. A little house; a cat; all she needed was a canary.

But all he said was, 'Nice,' as Catherine riffled through her wardrobe for something he could wear while his clothes were drying.

'The—er—bathroom's there,' she said, moving round him again, and pointing to the half open door. 'You can—take a shower, if you'd like to. In fact, that might be a good idea. To—er—to ward off a chill.'

Morgan's lips twisted. 'You're determined I'm going to catch a cold, aren't you,' he remarked, taking the peach-coloured towelling robe she gave him with a wry look. 'I'm not that fragile, you know. But I may just take you up on that shower. I guess I do feel kind of messy.'

'Help yourself.' Catherine turned away from him to slip off her coat, and then started when it was taken from her hands. 'Oh—thanks.' She moistened her dry lips. 'There are plenty of towels on the rack. I'll—er—I'll just go and let Hector out.'

Morgan laid her coat on the bed, and looked down at his rain-streaked trousers. 'What should I do with these?'

Catherine swallowed and adjusted her spectacles. 'Oh—just bring them down when you're finished,' she said, not liking her immediate reaction to his words. 'I'll—make some coffee.'

'Fine.'

He pulled his tie from around his neck, and, half afraid he was going to take his clothes off in the bedroom, Catherine hurried out on to the landing. It was ridiculous, she told herself, as she went down the stairs. It wasn't as if a man's naked body was any novelty to her, and yet she was behaving like an outraged virgin. For heaven's sake, Morgan might be taller, and more powerfully built, but the permutations were the same.

Even so, she couldn't help images of him taking a
shower in her bath from invading her mind. She could
see him lathering himself with her jasmine-scented soap,
washing his hair with her moisturising shampoo; drying
himself on her fluffy cotton towels. They would all have
to be washed, of course. She couldn't run the risk of
using a towel he had used, of smelling his distinctively
male fragrance...

CHAPTER THREE

HECTOR was awkward about going out, and in the end Catherine lost patience, and scooped him up and put him outside. She regretted it immediately. She was allowing her nervousness about Morgan Lynch to influence her dealings with the cat, and she guessed he would be feeling pretty huffy about it when he came back in.

Morgan's jacket was still lying on the table, and she picked it up to hang over the radiator. It wasn't the way a jacket of its quality should be dried, she supposed, but she didn't have much alternative. Besides, Morgan evidently didn't care that he had risked ruining it by walking in the rain, so why should she worry?

However, the weight of it warned her that the pockets were not empty, and, flipping it open, she discovered a long black wallet in the inside pocket. She hesitated before taking it out, and putting it down on the table. Emptying his pockets smacked of prying, and she didn't want him to think she had lured him here for any questionable reason.

The jingle of coins warned her that if she turned the jacket sideways, as she had intended to do, they would all spill out on to the floor. She hesitated, briefly, and then plunged her hand inside, and dumped the contents of his other pockets on the table, beside the wallet.

There were several coins, and some notes, as well as keys, a handkerchief, and a small bottle of coloured capsules that looked like medication. The temptation to read the inscription on the bottle was almost irresistible, but she resisted it, and, shaking the coat out, she draped it over the hot radiator.

42

The kettle had boiled, and the dark liquid was filtering through the grains when she heard Morgan coming downstairs. He was moving silently, but the stairs were inclined to creak. Immediately, her hands felt all thumbs, and she had to steel herself to continue setting out mugs, and a cream jug, and a small basin of dark brown sugar.

As she had expected, he had washed his hair, but, although he had towelled it dry, he had evidently not used her brush or comb. It was a dark tangled mass that somehow managed to give him a look of tumbled sensuality. The towelling robe didn't look too bad. Although it gaped a little across his chest, exposing the darkly tanned skin beneath, its length reached below his knees. However, his legs and feet were bare, and she tried not to think about the fact that he was carrying the rest of his clothes.

'Um—let me take those,' she said, when he halted in the doorway, his eyes going automatically to the small pile of his belongings on the kitchen table. 'I—er—I hope you don't mind. I've put your jacket over the radiator.'

Morgan's mouth compressed. 'Why not?' he said, though there was a certain tightness in his tone. He handed over his shirt, waistcoat, trousers, socks, and the scrap of grey silk which she guessed was his underpants. 'Thanks.'

Although the clothes were wet, the scent of his body lingered on them, and Catherine could smell it on her fingers, even after she had hung the trousers and waistcoat beside the jacket, and pushed the other garments into the tumble dryer. She thought of washing her hands, but that would have looked too obvious. Besides, it wasn't an unpleasant smell. On the contrary, it was disturbingly appealing.

'We'll—er—we'll have our coffee in the living room,' she said now, filling the mugs and adding them to the other items on a lacquered tray. 'You know the way,' she added, as Hector's voice could be heard, demanding entry at the front door.

'Do you want I should let him in?' Morgan asked, as Catherine's hands were full, and she sighed.

'I—if you wouldn't mind,' she agreed, silently cursing Hector for not staying in the back garden. She just hoped no one was about. It wasn't late, but hopefully the weather would have deterred people from turning out.

Morgan walked along the hall to the door, and lifted the latch. He moved easily for such a big man, and, to distract herself from her thoughts, Catherine tried to drum up a feeling of resentment at his familiarity. Really, she thought, anyone seeing him would imagine he was staying with her. And, while she was responsible for him being here, she couldn't help feeling aggrieved. She didn't want to get involved again, however fleetingly, with anyone. And, although she guessed that a man like Morgan Lynch was unlikely to be attracted to her in the normal way, she had no intention of being used, not even as a sexual stop-gap.

A draught of cold air wafted into the hall as Morgan opened the door. And Hector, after discovering it was not his mistress who had let him in, gave Catherine a disdainful look before padding into the living-room. Of course, he was wet, she thought, guiltily remembering she hadn't thought of that when she'd put him out. He had probably come round to the front, to shelter under the canopy. Oh, dear, she had probably offended him, too.

Morgan closed the door again, and as he came back along the hall Catherine quickly followed Hector into the living-room. Setting the tray on the low table before the hearth, she switched on a couple of lamps, and carefully positioned herself in an armchair. That way, he could have the sofa to himself, she thought decisively.

Hector was hovering on the hearthrug, his tail still up, and swishing slowly from side to side. He didn't have a long tail, but he made good use of what he had. He watched Catherine balefully as she sat down in the chintz-covered armchair.

Morgan grinned, all tension leaving his expression, as he seated himself on the sofa, at right angles to her chair. 'I guess that's what you call the evil eye,' he observed, spreading his legs and allowing his hands to hang loosely between.

'I suppose it is.'

Catherine forced herself to respond, and concentrated on the tray in front of her. But her eyes were drawn to the shadowed length of hairy leg visible in the opening of the bathrobe. He was completely unselfconscious, she thought, angry with herself for noticing. He didn't seem to care about what constituted a breach of etiquette and what didn't. He was totally unaware of his body, and she was a fool to be disturbed by it.

After setting his mug of coffee beside him, Catherine eased herself back in the chair, and crossed her legs. Perhaps it would encourage him to do the same, she thought, peevishly, but it didn't. He merely remained where he was, drinking his coffee, and studying his surroundings with a lazily interested eye.

His eyes were like Hector's, she noticed unwillingly. Until now, they had invariably been veiled by his dark lashes, but as he looked up, she saw that they weren't brown, as she had imagined, but a curious shade of amber. Cat's eyes, she thought fancifully, considering the comparison. In fact, he was not unlike Hector in the way he moved. They both shared a sinuous grace that lesser mortals coveted. And they both had the same God-given belief in their own supremacy, she reflected dourly, pursing her lips.

'Did I say something wrong?' he asked suddenly, and Catherine blinked behind her large lenses.

'No. Why?'

'You just looked kind of grim, that's all,' he responded, putting down his mug. 'I guess I didn't thank you for bringing me here.'

'You don't have to thank me.'

Catherine's voice was crisp, and she knew it. But she couldn't help it. The truth was, it troubled her to see him looking so at home on *her* sofa. As if he belonged there, she thought tensely.

He moved then, but, although she automatically stiffened, all he did was settle back against the cushions. And Hector—the *traitor*, she thought disgustedly— Hector walked delicately across the floor, and jumped up on to the sofa beside him.

Deciding she was allowing her reactions to this man to get completely out of hand, Catherine ran her tongue over her dry lips, and then said, woodenly, 'I understand you work at the Embassy, too. It must be interesting. Have you—have you worked in other countries?'

Hector was presently employed in settling himself on Morgan's knee, and Morgan ran his hand along the whole length of the cat's arching spine before replying. 'Some,' he conceded at last, non-committally. Then, 'You never did tell me what an investment analyst does. Do you work for the stock exchange?'

Catherine's lips tightened. It was obvious he didn't like talking about himself. This was the second time he had turned her questions against her, and, in spite of her determination not to get involved with this man, her curiosity was piqued.

'I'm employed by an insurance company,' she said now. 'I study the economy, and make recommendations about investments. I'm sure you'd find it very boring.' She paused. 'Not at all glamorous, like the diplomatic service.'

Morgan's hand paused midway along Hector's back. 'I'm not a diplomat,' he said flatly. He drew a considering breath, and then continued, 'I guess you compare the performances of different industries, don't you? So that pension schemes give good returns, that sort of thing.'

She was surprised at his understanding of her job, but she refused to let him divert her. 'That's right,' she said, dismissing the topic. 'So—if you're not a diplomat, what do you do? I thought Kay said you worked in Denzil's section.'

'I do.' Morgan expelled a heavy breath, watching how Hector's fur rose between his fingers as his hand moved along the animal's spine. 'I guess you could say I'm a general dogsbody,' he added, and when his eyes lifted to Catherine's face, she felt impaled by their chilling penetration. 'Does that satisfy you? Or would you like to know exactly how I spend my days?'

Catherine felt a wave of heat envelop her. 'I wasn't— that is—I'm sorry if you think I was—prying. I'm— interested, that's all.' She took a steadying breath. 'You didn't *have* to answer me.'

'Didn't I?' A little of the coldness left his face, but his mouth took on a half-contemptuous slant. 'And if I hadn't answered you, you'd have left it there, right?'

Catherine's free hand moved nervously to the silky black hair at the back of her neck. Her hair was straight, unflatteringly so, she sometimes thought, but it was decently cut, and tilted under slightly where it brushed her shoulders. Just now, it provided a suitable support to hold on to, and she met his sardonic stare with some defiance.

'You can ask questions about me, but I can't ask questions about you, is that right?' she asked, amazed at her own audacity, and he held her gaze for only a moment longer, before giving a rueful snort.

'Something like that,' he agreed, and now she sensed that his contempt was directed towards himself. 'Let's just say I'm a man of mystery, hmm?'

'Like Houdini?' suggested Catherine quickly, her voice a little unsteady with relief, but Morgan shook his head.

'More like the Phantom of the Opera,' he remarked, wincing as Hector tried his claws against his bare leg. He studied the cat for a while, and then said quietly, 'Do you ever go to the theatre?'

Catherine leant forward to put her coffee mug back on the tray. 'Not—usually,' she admitted, wondering what he would think if she told him how insular she had become since Neil walked out. 'I—don't go out a lot.' Which had to be the understatement of the year!

'Would you? If I invited you?' he asked, still looking at Hector, and Catherine caught her breath.

'What?' she mumbled, playing for time. 'Go—to the theatre with you?' She shook her head foolishly. 'When?'

Morgan looked up then, his tawny eyes strangely wary. 'Whenever,' he said, holding her gaze. 'Would you?'

Catherine swallowed. She was not prepared for this. The last thing she had expected was for Morgan Lynch to invite her out. She wasn't his type. She wasn't anyone's type, let's face it, she thought bitterly. Particularly not a man who, for all his claims of being a dogsbody, wore expensive suits, and looked like every woman's sexual fantasy. He wasn't interested in her. Not really. If she hadn't practically kidnapped him and brought him here, she doubted they would have even seen one another again, let alone made a date. For some reason, he must feel he owed her something. Maybe he felt obliged to make some kind of offer, because, whether he had wanted it or not, she had rescued him from the rain. Yes, that had to be it. He probably felt sorry for her. Well, she didn't need his sympathy. She was quite capable of finding someone to take her out, if she ever felt the need to do so.

Now, uncrossing her legs, she linked her hands together on her knees. 'It's very kind of you,' she began, choosing her words with care, 'but——'

'You'll take a raincheck, right?' Morgan finished the sentence for her, his tone ironic, and, although they weren't quite the words she would have used, Catherine nodded.

'I—er—I'd better go and see how your clothes are getting on,' she said, getting to her feet. 'You—you finish your coffee. I won't be a minute.'

In actual fact, she was several minutes. By the time she had let herself out of the sitting-room and walked the few yards to the kitchen, Catherine was shaking quite badly, and she took quite a while to gather her composure. It had taken some courage to turn him down, not least because she really hadn't wanted to do it. If she was honest with herself, she had to admit that the idea of going out with Morgan was compulsively appealing. And it wasn't just because she thought he might be feeling sorry for her that she had turned him down. It was because she sensed how dangerous it would be for her to get involved with a man like him—a man who looked like an angel, but who was probably a devil in disguise. She was attracted to him. There was no denying that. But something told her the risks were too great; that Morgan Lynch could hurt her far more than Neil had ever done.

When she eventually pulled herself together sufficiently to remember why she had come out to the kitchen in the first place, Catherine drew a breath, and moved over to the radiator to examine his coat and waistcoat and trousers. Lifting the trousers off the radiator, she discovered that they at least were virtually dry, but the shoulders of his jacket were still damp. But not damp enough to prevent him wearing it, she thought, hardening her heart. And, as the dryer had already switched itself off, his shirt, socks and underpants had to be dry, too.

And they were, the shirt sliding silkily between her fingers, so that she was made inescapably aware of its quality. On impulse, she brought the soft fabric to her cheek, rubbing it against her skin. It was deliciously sensuous, and it was only when she felt her lips turning against its smoothness that she thrust it away from her. God in heaven, what was she doing? she asked herself disgustedly. It was only a shirt, after all. She had silk shirts of her own.

Deciding the jacket might as well stay on the radiator as long as possible, she folded the other garments over her arm, and walked back to the sitting-room. A glance at her watch had alerted her to the fact that it was already half-past eleven. Late enough for someone who had to be up at seven-thirty tomorrow morning. Indeed, it was at least an hour later than she usually went to bed—though she had no intention of telling him that.

However, when she opened the sitting-room door, she realised that telling Morgan anything would be purely academic. In her absence, he had shifted his position, and now he was stretched out on the sofa, fast asleep. Asleep, she thought frustratedly, with Hector curled confidingly into the curve of his hip.

Her first impulse was to slam the door and wake him up. But she was not naturally a spiteful person, and a closer inspection of his supine form revealed the unexpected evidence of exhaustion in his face. There were dark hollows beneath the silky fringe of his lashes, she saw now, and a certain weariness to his expression that wasn't entirely erased, even in sleep. He looked... She sought for a word to describe him, and could only come up with one—vulnerable.

But that was ridiculous, she chided herself impatiently. There was nothing remotely vulnerable about Morgan Lynch. It was just her imagination working overtime, as usual. And yet, that world-weary tiredness was not faked. It couldn't be. Not when he was unconscious. So, for some reason, he must find it difficult to sleep in his own bed.

It wasn't until she had shooed Hector out of the room, and covered her unwanted houseguest with a warm quilt before seeking the sanctuary of her own bed, that Catherine thought of an alternative solution. Curling her toes into the cuffs of her satin pyjamas, she reflected that it was quite possible he had been burning the candle fairly continuously since he came to London. A man alone, with no wife or girlfriend to curtail his activities, he probably slept in a different bed every night.

She found this thought so unpalatable that it was at least another hour before she got to sleep herself. And when, in the early hours of the morning, Hector came to warm her toes, she unkindly kicked him off. After all, he hadn't proved himself to be much of a judge of character, she thought uncharitably. He had been quite prepared to switch his affections when it had suited him.

It was still dark, though not as dark as it had been, when Hector started to howl. At first, Catherine thought he was protesting because she had kicked him off the bed, but then she discovered he was still on the bed, though not in his usual position. Instead, she could see his outline at the foot of the mattress, tail up, back arched, in his most aggressive stance, and her spine tingled at the thought of what might have caused his agitation.

'Ssh,' she said, rolling over and reaching for her spectacles. Sliding them on to her nose, she struggled to sit up. She had been sound asleep and it wasn't easy to pull herself together. She couldn't imagine what could be the cause of his distress, and, while she tried to convince herself that she couldn't have an intruder at five o'clock in the morning, Hector's howls were not abating.

She was wondering whether she should switch on a light when she heard it. Over and above the cat's squalling, she could hear another sound, one equally as nerve-tingling, and her blood froze. It was a man's voice, of that she was fairly certain. But the unearthly sounds it was making were barely human.

And then she remembered who was occupying her sofa downstairs. Morgan Lynch. Swallowing, she reached for the lamp, and turned it on. Was it possible that he was making that noise? Dear God! She shivered uncontrollably. What kind of man was he? Was he really mad, after all?

She thought of hammering on the wall for help, but the Tollands on one side of her were away, and she wasn't keen on waking up the Randalls. She hardly knew them anyway, and what she did know was not encouraging. Mrs Randall was the kind of woman who subjugated her needs to those of her husband, and pretended she wouldn't have it any other way. And, although Mr Randall didn't actually beat his wife—at least, Catherine had never heard him doing so—he did treat her with a certain amount of contempt. He was not somebody Catherine would choose to run to in a situation like this, and, realising she couldn't just sit there and let Morgan wake the whole neighbourhood, she swung her legs reluctantly over the side of the bed.

Hector leapt off the bed and accompanied her, as she opened the bedroom door and padded to the top of the stairs. His bristling presence was not exactly supportive, but at least he had stopped his noisy protest. However, it meant that the sounds from downstairs were that much louder now, and, not knowing what to expect, Catherine started down.

Hector ran ahead of her as they reached the bottom, but Catherine's legs were not so steady. Indeed, they were decidedly unsteady, and belatedly she remembered that she hadn't put on her dressing-gown. Not that she was cold. On the contrary, she was perspiring quite freely. But still...

At least the sitting-room door was closed, she saw as Hector paced angrily before it. She had half expected

Morgan to be systematically laying waste to the house, and, now that she was downstairs, the front door was infinitely more appealing. She could just grab a coat and rush out into the street, she thought. There were people who would help her not a dozen yards away. The Scotts, for example. Oh, Mrs Scott was inclined to be nosy, but what did that matter, if the choice was between life and death? Would she rather be embarrassed and alive, or a conservative corpse?

The harrowing sounds went on, and she drew a trembling breath. It was like some sort of ritual keening, she thought, trying to be rational about it. The rise and fall of cadence had all the anguish of a lament, and yet there was a harshness to its tone that was more savage than mournful. Whatever it was, it scared the hell out of her, and, for the first time in her life, she wished she had a weapon of some sort to defend herself.

And then the noise stopped. Abruptly, without any warning, the sounds were cut off, and their place was taken by an eerie silence. Catherine swallowed, and she heard its echo with almost deafening resonance. Even Hector stopped his pacing to stare at her with accusing yellow eyes, and she shook her head in a gesture of helpless indignation.

But what now? What should she do? Go back upstairs to bed, and pretend she hadn't heard anything? Was that what Morgan would expect her to do? Perhaps he had heard her coming down the stairs, although how he could have done in the circumstances was beyond her. Whatever, she would probably be well-advised to do just that. There was no point in courting trouble—or danger either, for that matter.

But she didn't. No matter how sensible it might seem to avoid a confrontation, she couldn't go back upstairs without finding out exactly what had been going on. This was her house, after all, she told herself defensively. He had no right to behave as if it was a lunatic asylum. Besides, she was very much afraid that if she went back upstairs now the noise might start all over again. And she didn't think she would have the courage to come downstairs a second time.

Acknowledging Hector's impatient stance, she trod along the hall to the sitting-room door and halted. Should she knock, she wondered, or was that just another attempt on the part of her subconscious to delay the evil moment? It did seem ridiculous to think about knocking, when for the past goodness knew how long Morgan had shown absolutely no consideration for her feelings whatsoever.

Taking every bit of courage she had in her hands, she put her fingers on the handle of the door and turned it. Darkness. Beyond the door, no flicker of light was visible, and, with trembling fingers, she reached for the hall light switch and turned it on.

Immediately, the interior of the sitting-room was dimly illuminated, and as her eyes adjusted themselves to the light she saw that Morgan was, amazingly, where she had left him. The only difference was that the quilt she had thrown over him was now on the floor, but otherwise he didn't appear to have moved.

She licked her dry lips, her thoughts racing. Was it possible that what she had heard was his reaction to a nightmare? Was it conceivable that he had been unaware of what he was doing?

She could hardly believe it. But what other solution was there? He certainly seemed to be asleep now, and her heartbeats steadied at the thought that there could be some reasonable explanation for all this.

Hector had slipped into the room when she opened the door, and, although he hadn't resumed his previous position on the sofa, Catherine knew she couldn't leave him in there. It was possible that Morgan had awakened earlier, and he would know Hector hadn't been in there then. So perhaps it was unwise to pose the question now as to how he had returned.

Her bare toes curling into the soft carpet, Catherine tiptoed across the floor to where Hector was standing on the tumbled quilt. 'Come on,' she whispered, over-poweringly aware of the sound of Morgan's harsh breathing, as she tipped the cat off the quilt and picked it up. But when she moved to cover the man on the couch with the quilt, her attention was caught by the sight of Morgan's face. Even in the diffused light from the hall, it was impossible not to notice the beads of sweat stand-ing on his forehead, or the moist strands of hair that lay against his neck. Although his skin was dark, it was oddly pale, and even the skin of his chest, bared by the parting lapels of the bathrobe, was obviously damp.

Catherine only hesitated a moment before putting out her hand and touching his brow. It was cold, and clammy, and she looked around the room in dismay. But it wasn't cold. Certainly not cold enough to induce symptoms of this sort, and she was nervously fingering her spectacles when he spoke.

'What time is it?'

Catherine jumped, and even Hector gave an in-dignant growl. After the horrifying sounds of the last fifteen minutes, to hear Morgan speak in a perfectly normal voice was almost unnerving in itself, and Catherine could only stare at him in mute consternation.

Morgan stared at her, too, uncomprehendingly at first, and then with slow recognition. Levering himself up on one elbow, he ran the palm of his other hand down his cheek. It came away soaked with his own sweat, and he uttered a groan before sinking back against the cushions. 'God, I guess I went to sleep, right?'

Catherine nodded. Pushing the silky black hair that brushed the collar of her pyjamas behind her ears, she took a hasty look at the clock on the mantelpiece. 'It—it's half-past five,' she said, holding the quilt in front

of her, as if it was a shield. She moistened her lips. 'Are—
are you all right?'

Morgan drew a deep breath, before looking up at her
through the thick veil of his lashes. 'Did I wake you?'
he asked, without answering her.

'Er—I think so,' she admitted awkwardly, and, when
he made another sound of protest, and drew up one leg
so that the bathrobe fell apart across his thighs, she
quickly thrust the quilt down on top of him. But not
quickly enough, she acknowledged, the memory of hair-
roughened limbs indelibly imprinted on her mind.

Morgan's features twisted. 'What did I do? What did
you hear?'

Catherine, bereft of the quilt, felt unbearably exposed. 'Er—oh, nothing much,' she lied, unable to tell
him the truth. Not now. 'I—er—Hector woke me, actually. He—he hears everything. Any—any small sound.'

'Or any loud one, right?' Morgan continued drily. He
groaned again, and raked the nails of both hands across
his scalp. 'Hell, I'm sorry. I shouldn't be here. Why
didn't you just wake me up and send me on my way?'

Catherine half turned towards the door. 'It doesn't
matter,' she said, uncomfortably aware of her own
body's reaction, both to the shock of his recovery, and
his sensuality. Even in a situation like this, macabre as
it was, she couldn't help being aware of him, and the
feelings he engendered. But turning sideways only threw
the thrusting arousal of her full breasts into profile and,
not for the first time, she wished her breasts were small
and insignificant.

'I'll go now,' Morgan said abruptly, pushing the quilt
aside, and putting his feet to the floor. 'If you could
just tell me where my clothes are——'

'You can't go like that!' The words were out before
Catherine could prevent them, but, in any case, she didn't
want to retract them. He couldn't go in that state. He
was as much in danger of getting pneumonia now as he

had been earlier, and she told herself it was her conscience that insisted on doing the right thing. 'I—I'll make some coffee,' she said, reaching the doorway and looking back at him over her shoulder. 'Why—why don't you take another shower? There's plenty of hot water.'

CHAPTER FOUR

CATHERINE was trying to estimate the relative advantages of choosing Micro-Bite Electronics over Hereward Industries when Kay stopped beside her desk. The other woman looked vaguely embarrassed, and she offered Catherine a rueful smile, before saying awkwardly, 'Sorry about last night.'

Realising she was not giving the calculation her full attention in any case, Catherine pushed her spectacles up her nose, and looked at her friend with tired eyes. 'What?' she asked, hoping Kay wasn't about to indulge in a long post-mortem. After approximately four hours of sleep, she was in no mood to be charitable. However, it was not in her nature to be completely ungracious, and, lifting her shoulders, she said, 'It doesn't matter.'

'It does matter.' Kay evidently did want to talk, and, after a swift glance around her, she perched on the edge of Catherine's desk. 'I'd never have invited you if I'd known he was going to be so objectionable.'

Catherine sighed. 'So what's new?' she replied drily, surprised that Kay was prepared to criticise her husband so openly. 'Denzil and I have never——'

'Not Denzil, silly!' Kay slid off the desk in her impatience. 'Morgan, of course. Morgan Lynch. Honestly, the way he spoke to Denzil, I just wanted to die!'

Catherine's eyes narrowed. 'You don't think he deserved it?' she remarked slowly.

'Who? Denzil?' And when Catherine's silence provided her answer, Kay snorted. 'Of course not. You know what Denzil's like. He just—teases you, that's all. There was no need for Morgan to come to your defence like a bull at a gate! For heaven's sake, the evening was hard enough without him making it any harder!'

Catherine drew her lower lip between her teeth. 'So—why did you invite him?' she enquired softly, and saw the way the colour came into the other woman's cheeks at her words.

'Oh—as I said the other day, he's an old army friend of Denzil's.'

'Friend?' Catherine looked sceptical.

'Well, all right. Not—friend, exactly.' Kay hesitated. 'As a matter of fact, they're cousins. Only second cousins,' she added swiftly. 'But family is family, isn't it? You can't choose your relations.'

'No.' Catherine was fairly sure Morgan felt the same.

'Anyway,' went on Kay defensively, 'at least it got you out of your shell for the evening. And you have to admit, Morgan is pretty devastating to look at, isn't he? It's just a pity he—— '

She broke off abruptly, but there was no mistaking her agitation now, as she ran nervous fingers into the blonde curls at her nape. It was obvious she regretted starting such an ambiguous statement, and, turning her head from side to side, she pretended to be admiring her reflection in the windowed wall that divided the office.

Catherine let her believe she had got away with it for a few moments, and then she said quietly, 'It's just a pity he—what? What were you going to say?'

'What?' Kay turned to look at her with deceptively innocent eyes.

'You didn't finish what you started to say,' Catherine responded smoothly. 'About Morgan. Why is it a pity?'

'Oh...' Kay licked her lips, playing for time. 'Did I say that?'

'You know you did.' Catherine was terse.

'Oh, well—I just meant—it was a pity the evening ended as it did,' declared Kay, her words gathering speed and conviction, as she realised she had found an escape route. 'I mean, imagine walking home in all that rain! He must be m—stupid. *Stupid!*' She uttered an embarrassed little laugh, and looked at the watch on her wrist. 'Goodness, is that the time? I'd better go. I don't want to get into Mr Hollingsworth's black books today. Denzil's taking me to Paris for the weekend, and I want to ask if I can have Monday off.' She pulled a face. 'See you.'

Catherine nodded. 'Have a nice weekend,' she said, well aware that Kay was not being completely honest with her. But then, remembering her own dealings with Morgan, she wondered if she wasn't being silly. She didn't even have that excuse.

Catherine looked back at her computer, trying to make some sense of the spreadsheet of net present values, but it was just a confusing jumble of figures, the projected balance sheets she had prepared the day before providing no elucidation whatsoever. She was afloat on a sea of corporate information that for some reason refused to clarify itself.

Resting her elbows on the desk, she massaged her temples with long, slim fingers. Her spectacles slipped down her nose, but she didn't bother to replace them. Her head ached with the effort of trying to concentrate when her mind simply wasn't on her work. It was a new experience for her, and one she didn't appreciate in the slightest.

It was Morgan Lynch's fault, of course, she acknowledged. In spite of her defence of him to Kay, she was in no doubt that he was responsible for her present lack of concentration. And not just because, in one way or another, he had kept her awake half the night.

She wondered what Kay would have said if she had told her that Morgan hadn't walked home at all. That he had, in fact, spent the night at her house. God, she could imagine the speculation that would have caused! Not least because Kay would never believe nothing had happened. Well, nothing sexual anyway, thought Catherine wryly, tilting her head to rest her chin on her hands. As for what had happened—well, there was no way she could ever tell anyone about that. In fact, looking back on it now, she was half inclined to believe she had imagined the whole thing. But she hadn't!

She sighed. All the same, the whole incident had acquired the ambience of a bad dream, and she preferred not to think about it. But it wasn't easy putting it out of her mind when the man himself so persistently occupied her thoughts.

A shiver ran up her spine. Kay had been right about one thing, she thought reflectively. Morgan was just about the most devastating man she had ever seen. She had only to close her eyes to see the long dark lashes that veiled his curiously tawny eyes, the hard planes of his face, beneath the tautly drawn skin that covered his cheekbones. There was nothing soft about his face, and yet at times it was strangely beautiful, his mouth compressing over even white teeth.

She shook her head. She didn't like the feeling of not having control over her own thoughts. Even when Neil had left her, she had been able to find solace in her work. But just now she was finding it virtually impossible to do what she had to do, and, discovering it was almost lunchtime, she realised that she would probably have to spend her weekend catching up.

Leaving her desk, she walked across to the coffee machine, and punched in her requirements. Then, collecting the polystyrene cup, she carried it to the windows, looking down at the city through troubled eyes. As usual, on a Friday lunchtime, the streets below her were clogged with traffic. Lots of offices closed for the weekend at lunchtime on Fridays, and travel-weary commuters were struggling to make their way home. Thank goodness, she didn't have that problem, she thought wryly. Besides, the offices of Bracknell Associates, Insurance

Consultants, didn't close until five o'clock, a circumstance she had not really appreciated until today.

And why was that? she asked herself irritably. Why should she want to stay on at the office, when most of the staff couldn't wait to start their weekend? Why should she want to stay at her desk, when she was fortunate enough to have a comfortable home to go to?

She sipped her coffee with some impatience. The answer, she knew, involved Morgan Lynch, and it was unbearable that he should be having such a ridiculous effect on her life. But her home, in spite of its earlier association with Neil, had always been her refuge in times of trouble. After Neil had left her, she had made it over to her own design, and, since then, no man had invaded her territory. Morgan had changed all that, and while she could hardly accuse him of *invading*, he had—temporarily, she hoped—destroyed its peace and tranquillity.

But it wasn't just the atmosphere of the house that concerned her. After he had left that morning, she had systematically destroyed all trace of Morgan's occupation, even to the extent of throwing out a perfectly good half-full bottle of an expensive shampoo, simply because she suspected he had used it. She had even stripped the cover from the quilt she had used to cover him, and left a note for the woman who came in twice a week to clean for her to send it to the cleaners. Her desire to rid herself of any reminder of what had happened was almost paranoid, and that was what troubled her most.

And why? she asked herself frustratedly. What had he done, for God's sake? He hadn't even touched her.

She expelled her breath unsteadily. He hadn't had to, she acknowledged bitterly. She hadn't needed his participation to be aware of him in a way that bore no resemblance to her immature attraction to Neil. Just looking at him, she had suspected how unsatisfactory her relationship with her ex-husband must have been, and the rampant possibilities of that realisation were another part of her depression.

Of course, he didn't know any of this, she consoled herself firmly. At least, she hoped he didn't. Surely he could have read nothing sexual into the cup of coffee she had offered after his second shower? A cup of coffee he had declined, she remembered uneasily, recalling his brief but unequivocal refusal. He had come downstairs, a little less immaculately attired than earlier that evening, with the shadow of a night's growth of beard on his chin, but dressed and ready to leave. And apart from using her phone to call a minicab he had behaved as he had done earlier—he was polite, but curiously remote.

Which was probably why she was thinking about him now, she told herself forcefully. It wasn't that she had found him so overwhelmingly attractive at all. It was his—unpredictability that disturbed her. She was worried about him, that's all. Worried that, in some strange way, he wasn't exactly what he seemed.

What he seemed? Catherine stifled a groan. She really was getting paranoid about this. Morgan Lynch was exactly what he seemed—a good-looking, moderately wealthy man, with a steady if unexciting job at the Embassy. And he was perfectly capable of handling his own life. He didn't need her to worry about him.

All the same, she couldn't help associating what Kay had just said—or rather, what she *hadn't* said—with what had happened during the night. Had it been a nightmare? He hadn't actually told her. All he had done was apologise for disturbing her.

Her mother phoned soon after she got in from work that evening. Catherine had hardly taken off her coat and bent to greet Hector before the telephone rang, and she felt an immediate return of tension. Her thoughts leapt instantly to the possible identity of her caller, and it was with some reluctance that she lifted the receiver.

'Catherine? Is that you, darling? Have you been running?'

'Yes, and no.' Catherine endeavoured to regulate her breathing. 'I've just got in, actually. And—the phone startled me.'

'Oh, I see.'

Mrs Lambert seemed to accept her explanation, but, feeling the need to endorse what she had said, Catherine added, 'You don't usually phone at this time.'

'No.' Diverted now, her mother was more than willing to explain. 'I just wanted to confirm what day you're planning on coming down. Will it be Saturday or Sunday? I mean, as far as I'm concerned, you could come tonight, and spend the whole weekend, but I know you won't leave that animal of yours, will you?'

Catherine swallowed. She had completely forgotten saying she would go down to Oakley this weekend, and, with the amount of work she had brought home with her, she didn't really have the time. Besides, the last thing she needed at the moment was a cosy tête-à-tête with her mother.

'Catherine?'

Her silence had become noticeable, and, taking a deep breath, she said, 'I—hadn't really thought about it.'

'About what? When you're coming?'

'No.' Catherine hesitated. 'If.'

'But you said you would!' Mrs Lambert sounded hurt, and Catherine felt awful. After all, it wasn't her mother's fault that she had allowed thoughts of Morgan Lynch to distract her from her work.

'I've…just got such a lot to do,' she admitted lamely. 'I promised John I'd have some figures ready for him on Monday morning, and I'm not even halfway through the calculations.' She paused. 'I've had to bring them home with me.'

Mrs Lambert sucked in her breath. 'So, you're going to spend the whole weekend hunched over the computer?'

Catherine sighed. 'Something like that.'

'Well, I don't believe you.' Her mother sounded angry now. 'You weren't too busy to have dinner with the Sawyers, were you? I don't remember you worrying about any figures that evening. No, you were quite happy to oblige your friends, but when it comes to your mother——'

'All right. All right. I'll come.'

Catherine broke into the tirade to make her peace, and her mother gave a peevish sniff. 'You mean it?'

'Yes, I mean it.' Catherine considered for a moment. 'I'll come on Sunday. For lunch, if that's OK. That'll give me at least half the morning to work.'

Mrs Lambert sniffed again. 'You really are busy, then.'

Catherine suppressed her own irritation. 'I wasn't lying, Mother,' she said, realising it was only half the truth. In normal circumstances what she had to do could have been accomplished in a few hours. But these were not normal circumstances, and she wasn't absolutely sure how long it would take her.

'Very well.' Her mother hesitated for a moment, and Catherine prepared to ring off. But then, as if compelled by forces stronger than herself, Mrs Lambert added, 'Did—er—did you have a pleasant evening with Kay and Denzil?'

In other words, what was Denzil's army buddy like? thought Catherine impatiently. Which was probably the real reason her mother had rung. The ploy about which day she planned to visit had backfired, but Mrs Lambert was nothing if not tenacious.

'It was all right,' she said now. 'Kay's housekeeper made a cream cheese and asparagus mousse, and that was delicious. I'll have to get the recipe. I'm sure you'd like it.'

'I'm sure I would.' Mrs Lambert's tone was dry. 'Nothing exciting happened then, I gather.'

Catherine bit down hard on the flesh of her inner lip. 'No,' she replied tautly. 'Nothing exciting.'

'And—Denzil's friend? What did you call him? What was he like?'

Catherine's fingers tightened round the receiver. 'I'm not seeing him again, if that's what you mean,' she said, keeping her voice even with an effort. 'I'll see you on Sunday, Mother. Bye!'

She put down the phone before Mrs Lambert could say anything else, but after she had done so she experienced the usual sense of guilt at her lack of patience. After all, her mother was just being—motherly. Like all good parents, she wanted her daughter to be happy. The trouble was, her idea of happiness and her daughter's were not necessarily compatible.

Catherine spent the evening watching television. She knew there was no point in taxing her brain cells any more that day, and the undemanding procession of game shows, situation comedies, and drama that filled the screen were exactly what she needed to distract her thoughts. Of course, her eyes strayed often to the sofa, where Morgan had lain the night before, and just occasionally she thought she could still detect the aroma of his shaving lotion. But she was sure it was only her imagination, and she chided Hector when he stalked around the sofa, sniffing assiduously. She didn't want to be reminded that the cat had been as susceptible to Morgan's influence as she had herself.

Catherine slept fitfully, and awakened to the daunting realisation that she felt no more like work this morning than she had done the day before. But at least it wasn't raining, and already a watery sun was filtering through the blind in the kitchen.

After letting Hector into the garden, Catherine made a pot of coffee, and then settled down to read the morning newspaper. She would have her shower and get dressed later, she thought. If she started work at ten o'clock she could guarantee herself at least two hours before lunch. Of course, there was shopping to do. She generally went to the supermarket on Saturdays and stocked up for the week. She would have to do that this afternoon, and by then she would probably be glad of the break.

She was engrossed in a story about a Member of Parliament who had been accused of insider trading on the stock market when her doorbell rang. A glance at the kitchen clock informed her that it was barely nine o'clock, and, guessing it was probably the post, she put down her coffee-cup and went to answer it. She didn't give much thought to the fact that she wasn't dressed. She was sure the postman had seen far worse sights than her in the silky dragon-printed kimono which Aunt Agnes had brought her back from Tokyo. It was at least five years old, of course, and not really her sort of thing, but it was soft and comfortable, and she wasn't expecting any visitors. Unless her mother...

But, when she slid back the bolt and opened the door, it was neither the postman nor her mother who was standing on the step outside. A tall, dark-haired man dressed in faded jeans and a black leather jacket stood on the threshold, his attention momentarily distracted by a pair of motorists, who were having a noisy duel with their horns across the street. However, he had evidently heard the door opening, because he turned his head and looked at her, and Catherine caught her breath as she identified him.

'Hi,' said Morgan evenly. His tawny eyes made a disturbing appraisal of her appearance. 'Did I get you up?'

'What?' For a moment, Catherine was too shocked to answer him. Then, 'Oh—I—no. No. I was in the kitchen.'

'Right.' Morgan inclined his head. 'I guessed you'd be an early riser.'

'Did you?' Catherine wasn't sure she appreciated that comment.

'Yes.' Morgan glanced pointedly beyond her. 'Can I come in?'

Catherine tugged at the stem of her spectacles, which curled behind her right ear. 'Er—yes. Yes, I suppose so.' She stepped aside automatically, even though all her instincts were screaming at her to refuse. But she was very much aware of her vulnerability, standing there for anyone to see; and when Mrs Scott, across the road, came out to take in her milk she was glad to step back into the shadows. 'I—er—I was just having some coffee,' she added politely, making an effort to behave naturally. 'Would you like some?'

'Of your coffee?' queried Morgan, stepping past her into the hall. He pulled a wry face. 'Could you make that tea?'

Catherine frowned at him as she closed the door. 'Is there something wrong with my coffee?' she enquired coolly, and Morgan's face split into an irresistible grin.

'Well, let's say it—defies description,' he replied shamelessly, and then spiked any reply she might have felt compelled to make by bending to rub Hector's ears. The cat had come to see what was going on, and he made no demur when Morgan picked him up. 'How are you doing, boy? Met any sexy felines lately?'

Catherine's face suffused with colour as she brushed past him on her way to the kitchen. Just who did he think he was? she thought furiously. Coming here at this hour of the morning, and making sarcastic cracks about her coffee. Not to mention embarrassing her over Hector. They didn't know one another well enough for him to make personal remarks to her cat!

However, as she filled the kettle she had to admit that once again she was over-reacting. For heaven's sake, it wasn't as if Hector was going to be embarrassed. On the contrary, as she turned to plug in the kettle, Morgan paused in the doorway, with Hector purring and arching his back responsively against his hand. The little traitor had betrayed her again, she thought indignantly, jamming the end of the flex into the kettle with more force than intellect. He had never been half so friendly with anyone else.

'I guess you're not pleased to see me,' Morgan remarked after a moment, tipping the cat gently on to the floor, and propping his leather-clad shoulder against the jamb. 'Do you want me to go?'

Catherine, who had been clattering cups into saucers, and taking the teapot out of the cupboard, turned to give him a startled look. 'I—didn't say that,' she protested, uncomfortably aware of how shrewish she must appear to him. A proper old maid, she thought bitterly, discounting the fact that she had been married. After all, the marriage had broken up, and Neil had left her, not the other way about. If he didn't actually regard her as a spinster, he probably considered her the next best thing.

'You didn't have to,' Morgan said now, one brow arching with quizzical intent. 'Don't bother with the tea. I'm not thirsty. I just came to—well, to thank you, I guess. You don't have to entertain me. I'll leave right away.'

'No, I . . .' Catherine put out a hand as he straightened away from the door, and then allowed it to fall again when he turned to look at her. 'I mean—stay and have some tea. Please. I didn't mean to be—ungracious.'

She watched as he came back into the room, unable to prevent herself from stiffening as he came to lodge his hips against the table, not a yard away from where she was standing. But, crazy as it seemed, she knew she didn't want him to go, and her body suffused with heat as his eyes moved over her.

'Ungracious!' he said, whistling softly. 'Now, there's a word I've not heard in many a long year. And certainly never addressed to me. How can I refuse?'

Catherine allowed her breath to escape in shallow little gulps. She was intensely conscious of him lounging there, against her table, arms folded across his chest, his jacket falling open to reveal a faded denim shirt, unfastened at the neck. Her nervous gaze was drawn to the silver buckle that snared the belt that rode low on his hips. It seemed to be a representation of two snakes, wound together in a deathly embrace, but when her eyes drooped to the faded fly of his jeans, which tautly outlined the proof of his gender, she quickly tore her gaze away. Lord, what was wrong with her? she wondered sharply, turning to rest her hot palms on the cool steel of the drainer. Was she suffering some kind of mental aberration, or was this simply a case of premature senility?

'Who looks after the yard?' Morgan asked suddenly, and the draught of air against her neck warned her that he had come to stand behind her.

'The—the yard?' she echoed, through dry lips, and he made a wry sound.

'Oh, right,' he said. 'You call it the garden, don't you? So, OK, who looks after the garden? You?'

'Yes.' Catherine's voice was clipped, but she couldn't help it. 'I—er—there is no one else. It's not big enough to employ a gardener.'

'No.' Morgan agreed with her, but he didn't move away, and Catherine was aware of him with every nerve in her body. 'So, you go to work in the City, you do some gardening, and you look after our aristocratic friend here. What else do you do?'

Catherine swallowed, and edged sideways, so that he wasn't immediately behind her any more. 'Oh—this and that,' she replied, wishing the kettle would boil, so that she would have something practical to do. 'I read; and I watch television. And—I like the theatre.'

'How about men?' Morgan gave her a sidelong glance. 'I guess there's no man in your life, right?'

Catherine didn't know why, but she was suddenly furious at his presumption. 'Why—why should you think that?' she stuttered, realising she should have put on her shoes before answering the door. It wasn't usual for her to have to look up at a man, and Morgan was taller to begin with. She caught her breath. 'I suppose you think Kay and Denzil only invited me to make up a four for dinner, because they felt sorry for me! Is that it?'

Morgan's brows creased. 'Do you want to run that by me again?' he asked, his own expression hardening, but Catherine was too angry to notice his reaction.

'I am not a lonely old woman!' she declared, trembling with indignation. 'If I live alone, it's because I choose to do so, not because no red-blooded male has asked me to join him. Strange as it may seem, I find my own company quite satisfying, thank you. I don't need the kind of sexual stimulus most men consider indispensable!'

'Hey!' Morgan caught her arm, and swung her round to face him. 'What did I say, for God's sake?' His tawny eyes glittered angrily. 'Did I suggest you were either old or lonely?'

'No, but...'

Catherine made one abortive attempt to shake his hand from her arm, and then stood rigidly still. She would not behave like some outraged prude, she thought determinedly. She was a mature, independent woman, and indulging in any kind of physical by-play was alien to her. Besides, she had the sense to know that in any kind of contest of strength he was bound to come out the winner, and she had no intention of struggling with him, just to prove the point.

'What is it with you?' demanded Morgan harshly, and she wondered if he realised how painful his grip was. His hard fingers were biting into the soft flesh of her upper arm, and she could feel the muscles around them going numb. 'I was simply trying to find out if there was someone else—some other man,' he added, his mouth revealing an expression of contempt now, which could have been against her, or self-derogatory. 'Why would you assume I was taking a shot at you? You're a beautiful woman, for God's sake! And I guess you don't need me to tell you that either!'

A beautiful woman! Catherine opened her mouth to deny this outrageous statement, and then closed it again. But she knew she wasn't a beautiful woman, and he must know it, too. It was just an attempt to disarm her. However, she would not give him the satisfaction of arguing with him. If he chose to make exaggerated observations, then let him. She would show him how little it meant by not even acknowledging the fabrication.

'Will you let me go?' she asked instead, her features as frozen as the rest of her, and, as if just realising he was bruising her arm, Morgan's hand fell to his side.

'Sorry,' he muttered, in a low voice, watching as she backed away from him, the fingers of her other hand trying to massage some life back into her arm. He raked his scalp with a hand that she couldn't help noticing was not quite steady, and then walked rather stiffly round the table. 'I'll let myself out.'

This time, Catherine made no attempt to detain him, but, after she heard the front door close behind him, she scurried into the sitting-room, and peered rather anxiously through the curtains. She realised now that the sleek grey Mercedes parked at her gate, and which she had paid little attention to earlier, was his. As she watched, Morgan came out of her gate, and crossed the pavement, unlocking the car with a controlled movement, and folding his long length behind the wheel. Cars were often parked at her gate, but seldom a car as powerful as that, she thought grudingly. She drew back as he gave the house a cursory inspection before driving away. Thank goodness, he had gone. And after what had happened, she doubted he'd be back.

CHAPTER FIVE

THE flowers were waiting for her when she got home from work on Monday afternoon. They must have arrived while Mrs Holland was cleaning, for the daily woman had taken them in and left them in the sink, their stems safely dipped in water.

What Mrs Holland must have thought, Catherine couldn't imagine. She was not in the habit of receiving extravagant bouquets of flowers, and, bearing in mind the season, and the shortage of locally grown blooms, they were doubly surprising. There must have been at least a hundred pounds' worth of flowers spilling over the drainer, their perfume filling the house with the freshness of a spring morning.

There was no card. As soon as she had prepared Hector's evening meal, that was the first thing Catherine looked for, but there was no small square of cardboard to indicate who they had come from. Of course she knew the identity of the sender. That was why she had forced herself to feed the cat before confirming her suspicions. But, once again, Morgan had succeeded in out-manoeuvring her, leaving her almost certain she was right, but not quite.

Still, they were beautiful, she thought, touching the petals of a delicate mauve orchid. Roses and lilies, tulips and carnations, freesias—where on earth had they been cultivated? Not in Fulham, that was for sure.

Leaving Hector licking his paws, Catherine walked back along the hall to the stairs. The sight of the phone on the semi-circular table by the door momentarily distracted her, but she moved past it. She could hardly ring and thank him for flowers she didn't even know he had sent. Besides, she didn't know his phone number. Just 1805, Jermyn Gate, which might, or might not, be his address.

In spite of her most immediate problems, it was still a relief to shed her business clothes and high heels. Deciding to take her bath later, she removed her make-up and washed her face, and then dressed in black woolly tights and a sloppy sweatshirt. She was unaware of it, but in the casual clothes, without make-up, and with her hair cupping her chin like an ebony bell, she looked about nineteen, her spectacles only accentuating the youthful transparency of her skin.

However, Catherine felt every one of her thirty years as she went downstairs. It had not been a good day, she thought, returning to the kitchen to confront the daunting array of flowers. Let's face it, she added silently, it had not been a good weekend. Indeed, things had started badly with Morgan's arrival on Saturday morning, and had continued going downhill ever since. Even the flowers, beautiful as they undoubtedly were, could not lift the depression that had gripped her, ever since Morgan had walked out of the house. She had wanted him to go—of course she had, she told herself. But the fact remained that his departure had signalled the start of her depression, and it wasn't over yet.

It certainly hadn't helped her to concentrate. Saturday morning had been a complete waste of time, and, after doing her shopping, in the early afternoon, she had had to spend the rest of the day battling with the computer. She had made some progress, but not a lot, and being obliged to go to Oakley on Sunday for lunch had successfully ruined that day's concentration, too.

Her mother hadn't helped either. Mrs Lambert had been more interested in the evening she had spent at the Sawyers' than in her work, and when Catherine had mentioned her predicament her mother had swiftly put her straight.

'I've told you before, Catherine,' she said, taking their pre-packed lunches out of the oven, and setting them on the hob. Mrs Lambert had never enjoyed cooking, and since Catherine had got married she seldom, if ever, prepared a traditional Sunday lunch. 'You've made your work the most important thing in your life, and that's foolish. Heavens, I enjoy my independence as much as anyone, but I wouldn't dream of bringing my work home. A place for everything, and everything in its place, as your grandmother used to say. You need a man, Catherine. Whether you choose to admit it or not.'

Catherine could have said that, as a salesperson, Mrs Lambert couldn't very well bring her work home, even if she had wanted to, but she held her tongue. It was easier not to get involved in arguments of that kind. Besides, there was some truth in what her mother said. It wasn't necessary for her to work at home. If she chose to do so, that was her problem.

But, at the same time, she couldn't tell her mother why she needed to work this weekend. If she had been afraid that Kay might speculate over the news that Morgan had spent Thursday night at her house, how could she confide that fact to her mother? Mrs Lambert would read all sorts of interpretations into the reasons why her daughter had brought him home in the first place. It wouldn't do to simply say that she had given him a lift because it was raining, and that she hadn't been able to find his address. Her mother would insist on knowing every minute detail of the events of that evening, and she wouldn't rest until Catherine had been completely de-briefed. On top of that, there were certain things about that night that Catherine didn't feel she had the right to tell anyone, least of all someone like her mother.

Hoping to change the subject, she got up to take down the plates that had been warming above the oven. 'This looks interesting,' she said, indicating the individual foil dishes that appeared to contain a mixture of rice and fish. 'What is it?'

'It's salmon and prawn fricassee,' retorted her mother shortly, not at all pleased by Catherine's refusal to discuss her private life. 'I don't suppose it will suit you. Nothing I do ever does.'

Catherine sighed. 'Mother——'

'Well, it's true.' Any hope of avoiding the issue was dispelled as Mrs Lambert launched into her favourite topic. 'You never listen to anything I say. And when I show a perfectly natural interest in your affairs, you clam up.'

'I don't clam up,' protested Catherine wearily, but her mother was adamant.

'You do,' she said. 'Take last Thursday, for instance. You tell me I can't come over, because you're going to the Sawyers', but when I ask you about the evening all you can say is that Kay's housekeeper made some fancy mousse or other.'

'She did.'

'Yes. Well, don't you think that's rather strange? I mean, you spend a whole evening with the Sawyers and this man they've invited you to meet——'

'It wasn't like that!'

'And all I hear is what you've been eating!'

Catherine sighed. 'What do you want me to say?'

Her mother snorted. 'I want to hear about what happened, of course. I'd like to know what this man was like for a start. Why didn't you like him? Did he like you?'

'Oh, God!' Catherine sank down into a chair at the table, and pushed her fingers into her hair. 'I've told you. It wasn't that kind of arrangement. Kay needed somone to make up a four for dinner, and I obliged. End of story.'

Mrs Lambert stared at her penetratingly for a few seconds, and Catherine was beginning to wonder guiltily if her mother had added mind-reading to her other talents when she turned away to dish up the food.

'Well, I think you're wasting your life,' she said, her words bringing her daughter some relief. 'It's not as if Neil had died, or anything, and you could be excused on the grounds of being grief-stricken. The man walked out on you, Catherine. He's living it up now, with that bimbo he married, and you're going around in sack-cloth and ashes!'

'Hardly that.' Catherine was surprised at how little her mother's words touched her. A few days ago, she would have expected the reminder of Neil's infidelity to be painful to her. But it wasn't. All she felt now was a lingering sense of bitterness, at having wasted the years they spent together. She should have realised sooner how selfish Neil was, how basically insecure their marriage had been.

'Well, anyway,' went on her mother, 'I think you know what I'm getting at. It's probably why the Sawyers invited you to dinner, whatever you say. Kay must know how you keep to yourself. She no doubt invited this man because she hoped you'd hit it off.'

'It wasn't like that,' exclaimed Catherine again, her voice rising in frustration. 'For heaven's sake, Mum, men and women have been known to socialise with one another, without feeling the need to fall into bed!'

Of course, that had been the end of the discussion, but not of the argument. Catherine had left, after making a gallant attempt to swallow at least half of her share of the fricassee, knowing that Mrs Lambert was unlikely to be silenced for long. But at least she had avoided any more questions about Morgan. God willing, her mother

would have forgotten all about him, when next the subject of Catherine's single status came up.

Even so, she had not found it any easier to work when
she got back home, and this morning John Humphries,
her immediate superior, had been less than understanding over her unfinished report. Of course, she had
known that part of his ill humour stemmed from the
hangover he invariably had on Monday mornings, but
nevertheless his attitude hadn't helped to relieve her own
tension.

She ran out of vases long before she had accommo-
dated all the flowers. Instead, she was forced to use jugs,
and a wine cooler, even putting a tender bunch of freesias
into an ornamental teapot that was never used. When
she had finished there were flowers everywhere, and
Hector looked askance at the bowl she put in the downstairs cloakroom.

'Well,' she said defensively, 'you can't deny they
brighten up the place. And I can hardly send them back
when I don't know who's sent them, can I?' She
frowned. 'Why do you think he did it? What is he trying
to prove?'

Hector didn't have an answer. He only wound himself
about her legs, in his usual illustration of affection. Well,
camaraderie anyway, amended Catherine wryly, remembering how perfidious Hector could be.

She made herself an omelette and a salad for her
supper, and spent the rest of the evening waiting for the
telephone to ring. Either that, or the doorbell, she
anticipated, determining not to give in to the urge to go
and change her clothes. She didn't care what *he* thought
of her, she told herself grimly. She had no intention of
dressing up and putting on make-up, just on the off-
chance that *he* might call. She wished he hadn't started
it all up again by sending the flowers. She had been de-
pressed, it was true, but she would have got over it. She
had done so before. Besides which, her depression had

been mostly caused by guilt. Guilt she could cope with. Emotional involvements, on the other hand, were poison.

The phone rang as Catherine was taking a shower the next morning. She had put off taking her bath the night before, unwilling to take the chance that Morgan might ring. Oh, she had told herself it was because if he had sent the flowers she could tell him she was sending them right back to him. But whether she would actually do so was something she had refused to consider.

Nevertheless, when she frustratedly turned off the tap, snatched a towel from the rack, and tramped, dripping, across the bedroom carpet to answer it, the possibility that it might be Morgan didn't even occur to her. At this hour of the morning, she thought it was most likely her mother, ringing to inform her that in her haste to leave on Sunday she had forgotten the print that Fliss, the owner of the gallery where Mrs Lambert worked, had got for her. Catherine had remembered that the night before, too, but the idea of ringing her mother then had not borne thinking about.

Now, however, she was resigned to hearing another monologue about her shortcomings, and how ungrateful she was to someone who only had her best interests at heart, and when a male voice answered her rather weary, 'Hello?' she was too shocked for a moment to make any response.

'Miss Lambert? Catherine? I do have the right number, don't I?'

'Yes.' When Catherine did find her voice again, it was decidedly breathy. 'Er—Mr Lynch!'

'You got it. Mr Lynch,' he agreed drily. 'I hope I'm not interrupting anything.'

'Like what?' Catherine was instantly defensive, and she heard his rueful laugh.

'Hey, I don't know, do I?' he exclaimed. 'You could be having an orgy there. I'm not suggesting anything.'

Catherine felt a smile touch her lips in spite of herself. 'I—was having a shower, if you must know,' she told him, keeping her tone entirely neutral. 'What—what can I do for you?'

'Now, there's a question,' he countered, and, even without seeing him, she could imagine his dark sardonic face. 'You know, I may just need a little time to come up with an answer to that.'

Catherine drew in her breath. 'What do you want, Mr Lynch? I don't have a lot of time. I do have a job to go to, in case you've forgotten.'

'Oh, Miss Lambert, I've forgotten nothing about you, believe me.' Morgan's voice was low and to Catherine's ears, faintly mocking. 'You start at nine o'clock, right? That gives you—' there was a pause while she assumed he consulted his watch '—about another thirty-five minutes before you need to leave.'

Catherine's lips tightened. 'I thought you weren't familiar with London.'

'I'm not.' Morgan paused. 'I asked someone who is.'

'Not—Denzil?'

'Right.'

'Oh, lord!' Catherine made a sound of impatience. 'What did you have to ask him for?' she demanded, well aware that Kay was unlikely to let that juicy piece of gossip slip through her net. God! As if her mother's prurient curiosity had not been enough.

'I didn't,' remarked Morgan evenly. 'You said *not* Denzil, and I said right.'

Catherine snorted. 'You deliberately misled me,' she exclaimed, her annoyance at his confusing her momentarily outweighing her relief at knowing that Denzil had not been involved, and Morgan sucked in his breath.

'Hey, I'm not the one who's making the mistakes here,' he protested mildly. 'Just because you don't understand plain English——'

'Is that what you call it?' Catherine was scathing. 'I'd say that, like my coffee, your English defies description!'

'Is that so?' Morgan sounded thoughtful. 'Seems like you've not forgotten anything I've said either.'

'Don't flatter yourself!' Catherine was getting cold, but she was aware that the goose-bumps on her skin were not wholly caused by the temperature of her body. 'And—if the only reason you've called is to tell me you know how long it takes me to get to the office, do you mind if we continue this at some other time?'

'Does that mean you want to see me again?' Morgan enquired, the husky timbre of his voice sending little darts of fire along her veins, and Catherine struggled to remain calm.

'It means that if I don't hurry I'm going to be late,' she retorted, clutching the folds of the towel closer about her. 'Really, I don't think there's any point in——'

'Did you get my flowers?' he interrupted abruptly, and her knees sagged.

'I—got *some* flowers,' she admitted, allowing the backs of her legs to rest against the side of the bed. 'As they didn't have a card, I didn't know who they were from.'

'Ah.'

Morgan was silent for a moment, and reluctantly feeling obliged to make some concession, Catherine added stiffly, 'They were—they *are*—beautiful. But you shouldn't have done it.'

'Why not? Didn't you like them?'

'That's not the point...' Catherine's tongue circled her lips with some uncertainty. 'I mean—you shouldn't spend your money on me.'

'Is that how you see them?' Morgan's voice sounded cynical suddenly, and Catherine was reminded of other, not always comprehensible things he had said.

'No,' she said now. 'But—well—they must have been expensive.'

'Cost is relative,' replied Morgan flatly. 'As an investment analyst, you should know that.'

Catherine sighed. 'That doesn't alter the fact that——'

'You didn't want them, right?'

Catherine shook her head, and sank down on to the side of the bed. Her spectacles were lying on the table beside her bed, and, sliding them on to her nose, she took a steadying breath. Now was her chance to tell him exactly that: that she didn't want them, and, with his permission, she'd send them to the nearest hospital. But she didn't. When it came right down to it, she couldn't do it. She didn't *want* to do it, moreover. But—that didn't mean she had to get any more involved than she already was.

'Look,' she said, choosing her words carefully, 'no woman in her right mind would say she didn't want them. As I said before, they're... gorgeous! All I am saying——'

'Have lunch with me,' Morgan broke in bluntly, with another of his capricious changes of mood, and Catherine stared at the phone with dismay. Once again, he had totally swept the ground from under her, and, although she knew what her answer should be, it wasn't that easy to articulate it.

'I—I only get an hour for lunch,' she temporised, wondering why she was searching for an excuse. All she had to say was *no*. It was as simple as that.

'That's OK.' Before she could say any more, Morgan had accepted her statement as valid. 'I guess an hour is long enough. Is one o'clock all right?'

Catherine was tempted to say, 'Long enough for what?' but as her eyes focused on her bedside clock, she was shocked into action. 'I—I've got to go,' she said, and, putting down the receiver, she ended the conversation.

Of course, all the way to work, strap-hanging on the Underground, she worried over what she had done. She should have just said, no, one o'clock wasn't all right, and left it at that. She could even have hung up on him then, without fear of recrimination. But, instead, she hadn't given him an answer. She'd just put down the phone, like a scared rabbit, and hurried out of the house, in case he rang again.

Not that he hadn't had time to ring again, before she'd left Orchard Road, if he'd wanted to, she admitted reluctantly. After all, although she had forgone her own breakfast, she had had to provide Hector with his, and there had been her hair to dry, and her clothes to put on . . .

Oh, what the hell! she thought irritably, as she walked from the Tube station to the skyscraper block of offices in which Bracknell Associates occupied the top two floors. It didn't matter, either way. Morgan Lynch just found her amusing, that was all. It amused his distorted sense of humour to play with her, knowing that, in spite of her divorced status, she was unused to his kind of sophisticated baiting. No wonder Hector hadn't objected too strongly to his presence. He had probably recognised a kindred spirit, she thought sourly. Two predators, who enjoyed teasing their prey before destroying it.

Destroying it?

Catherine winced at her own exaggeration. For heaven's sake, Morgan had done nothing to warrant such a derogation of his character. As usual, she was overdramatising the situation. She was allowing the fact of her own unwanted infatuation with the man to colour his whole personality, and just because she didn't know how to handle her emotions was no excuse for allowing irrationality to overtake reason.

With this analysis of the situation firmly decided, Catherine settled down to work with renewed enthusiasm. She doubted she would hear from Morgan again. Apart from anything else, he didn't know where she worked. That was something she hadn't told him. Just that she was an investment analyst and nothing else. Analyst, analyse thyself, she misquoted drily, and fed another segment of projected interest rates into the computer.

She saw Kay briefly during the morning. Catherine came out of a cubicle in the ladies' washroom to find the other girl washing her hands at the sink. She thought Kay looked momentarily discomfited to see her, but she quickly recovered her composure, to say lightly, 'Did you miss me yesterday?'

'Miss you?' Catherine frowned, as she turned on the taps and Kay made a sound of indignation.

'Obviously, you didn't,' she declared, turning on the hand-dryer. 'Well, for your information, we had a marvellous weekend!'

'Oh—yes. You went to Paris.' There had been so many other things to think about that Catherine had completely forgotten what Kay had told her.

'That's right.' Kay hesitated now, but as if the lure of telling Catherine about her trip overcame any reticence she still felt about their fateful dinner party, she propped her hip against the wall. 'Oh, Cat, I can't tell you how exciting it was! You should have come with us.'

Catherine managed an envious grimace, as she dried her own hands, but she could imagine few things less attractive than a trip to Paris with Denzil Sawyer. Still, Kay had always had a blind spot where Denzil was concerned, and, after what had happened last week, Catherine had no intention of trying to expunge it. Instead, she listened politely to Kay's extravagant account of the restaurants they had visited, and the clothes she had bought, and eased her way carefully towards the door.

'Did you have a nice weekend?' Kay enquired at last, just as Catherine was about to make her excuses and leave, and she heaved a sigh.

'Oh—the usual,' she murmured, not wanting to get involved in a discussion about her activities. 'I—er—I went to Oakley on Sunday. That's about it.'

Kay nodded, rather smugly, Catherine thought, and then chided herself for being so sensitive. After all, it wasn't as if she envied Kay her Continental weekend. Just her naïveté about her marriage, perhaps, she admitted ruefully.

The morning passed surprisingly quickly. Somehow, after her chat with Kay, Catherine found it easier to concentrate, and it wasn't until the office started to empty at lunchtime that she realised she had used her dislike of Denzil to keep other thoughts at bay.

'Coming for a drink, Cath?' Melvin Scott, one of her colleagues, asked, stopping by her desk, and she looked up at him doubtfully.

'Oh—I don't know,' she murmured, her nerves prickling very slightly at the thought that Morgan might be outside, waiting for her. It wasn't likely, of course. In fact, it was highly unlikely. But leaving the building would make her vulnerable, and her nerves rebelled against it.

'Why not?' Melvin was a married man, not much older than herself, and in the ordinary way they had often enjoyed a drink and a sandwich together in the local pub. 'Come on,' he urged. 'Look, the sun's even shining. I know John wants those figures, but you're entitled to a break.'

Catherine hesitated. She was being silly, really. And she couldn't truly justify her reasons for refusing. As a matter of fact, the figures her superior wanted were almost ready for the print-out. He could have them after lunch, no problem.

'All right,' she said, giving in, and switching off the monitor, she got up from her chair. 'I'll just get my coat.'

It was a little after a quarter to one when they emerged from the building. The block of offices stood in a square, just off Cannon Street, and the pub they usually visited occupied the corner site. It wasn't far to walk, but Catherine was intensely conscious of every stationary vehicle as they crossed the square. But there was no grey Mercedes, and she breathed a little more easily as they reached the corner.

'Am I late?'

The words, spoken in that low, distinctive, drawl, brought Catherine up with a start, and Melvin's fair, good-looking face drew into a puzzled frown. They had actually reached the entrance to the pub, when the casually spoken enquiry arrested them, and they both turned to confront the man behind them.

Morgan looked infuriatingly relaxed as he faced them, his weight concentrated on his left leg, his hands thrust carelessly into the pockets of another immaculately styled jacket. Unlike Melvin, he was not wearing an overcoat over his navy-blue suit, and, feeling the wind whipping about her own shoulders, Catherine wondered at his apparent indifference to the elements.

Melvin was the first to speak. One glance at Catherine's shocked face had assured him that she was as surprised at this interception as he was, and, although it must have taken a considerable amount of courage to face down a man who was so much bigger than he was, he rallied to the occasion.

'Are you talking to us?' he asked, with some condescension in his tone, and Morgan's attractive mouth twisted.

'Not to you, friend,' replied Morgan, pleasantly enough. 'I was speaking to the lady. She and I have a date for lunch, don't we, Cat?'

Melvin blinked, and looked at Catherine, but, seeing no recognition in her face, he ploughed on. 'I don't think so,' he began, taking her arm and urging her into the smoke-filled atmosphere of the bar. But, before they had moved half a step, Morgan's hand fastened on his shoulder, and Melvin winced in obvious agony.

'I said, I was speaking to the lady,' Morgan repeated, his tone decidedly less than pleasant now, and, realising she couldn't allow this to go any further, Catherine released herself from Melvin's weakening grasp.

'It's all right, Mel, honestly,' she said, giving Morgan a brief, but killing glance. 'I—er—I'd forgotten about this.' She gave Melvin a gentle push towards the bar, so that Morgan was forced to let him go. 'Go ahead. Get your lunch. I—er—I may join you later.'

Melvin hesitated, rubbing his shoulder. 'Are you sure?'

'You heard the lady,' said Morgan, without emotion, and, much to Catherine's dismay, he slung his arm across her shoulders. 'Go on, Mel. Get your lunch. But don't hold your breath where Cat's concerned, will you?'

Catherine was furious, but she knew that if she showed her real feelings Melvin would feel obliged to defend her. And she didn't want that. Goodness, she could just imagine how embarrassing it would be, if Morgan chose to handle the situation his way. She didn't think Melvin's wife would appreciate having her husband come home with a black eye, *or worse*.

Forcing a rueful smile, she nodded, but as soon as Melvin had reluctantly entered the pub she dragged herself away from Morgan's possessive hold. 'How dare you?' she exclaimed, her anger sustaining her against the unwelcome wave of heat his touch had engendered. Just for a moment, she had been close against his hard body, and she was painfully aware that she hadn't really wanted to break free.

'Something wrong?' Morgan was maddeningly unruffled, though she glimpsed a trace of other emotions, swiftly controlled, in his cool amber gaze. He was not quite as unconcerned as he would have her believe, she thought, and it was to release this inner conflict that she allowed her temper free rein.

'You ask me that?' she blazed. 'What do you think you're doing, hanging about outside the office like some second-rate private eye? Threatening my friends! This is England, Mr Lynch. We don't behave like savages here!'

Morgan's features had hardened as she was speaking, but Catherine refused to be intimidated by his expression. Heavens, who did he think he was? Her keeper?

'Is that what you think I am?' he said at last, when she paused for breath, and, in spite of her outburst, Catherine was briefly speechless.

'I—what?' she said at last, moving out of the way of a group of accountants from the office, who looked at them both with evident curiosity as they filed into the pub.

'A savage,' said Morgan harshly, his mouth thinning to a fine line, and, although Catherine had just said it, she faltered over the endorsement.

'Well—you—weren't exactly polite, were you?' she mumbled, pushing her own hands into the deep pockets of her cashmere coat. She didn't know what the temperature was, but, in spite of the fact that the sun was still shining, she was freezing, and she was pretty sure Morgan must be, too. 'Oh, forget it,' she added, dipping her chin into her collar.

Morgan didn't move. 'Is that the current man in your life?' he asked, and if she hadn't felt so distracted Catherine thought she would have laughed.

'Mel?' she exclaimed. 'Melvin Scott?'

'If that's his name.'

Catherine sighed. 'Mel's a married man!'

'So?'

'So—no. No, of course he's not the current man in my life.' She bent her head. 'There is no—*current*—man, and you know it.'

'Do I?'

Morgan regarded her intently for a few moments, and Catherine felt every hair on her body rise. No, she told herself severely. No, this could not be happening. But it was—and when he put out his hand and gripped the back of her neck, she didn't resist as he pulled her towards him.

CHAPTER SIX

His mouth was firm and persuasive; not aggressive, as she had half expected, but warm and possessive, his tongue pressing insistently against her lips. Although she kept her hands in her pockets, she was aware of his nearness down the whole length of her body, and it took the utmost effort to keep her lips together. His free hand linked with the other, his thumbs tipping her face up to his. The touch of his admittedly cool hands on her warm skin caused shivers up and down her spine, but their familiarity sent flames of fire licking along her veins.

When he let her go, she stepped back in confusion, not entirely in control of her movements. Her glasses were steamed up, and she brushed them with an impatient hand. Morgan's lips tilted in knowing sympathy. 'Lunch, hmm?' he suggested, as Catherine became embarrassingly aware of her surroundings. She had no idea how many people had passed them while he was kissing her, but, judging by the amused faces at the windows of the pub, they had caused quite a spectacle.

'I...' She looked awkwardly around her. 'Oh—all right.' She gave in unwillingly. 'But I only have about three-quarters of an hour left.'

'That's OK.' Morgan shrugged, and held out his hand. 'Let's walk.'

In spite of her misgivings, which grew with every passing minute, Catherine went with him. But she didn't take his proffered hand. She kept her balled fists securely anchored in her pockets, and, with a careless shrug, he accepted the rebuff.

'You kiss like a virgin,' he said, after a few minutes, and Catherine could barely restrain her indignation.

'I'm sorry,' she said, her voice icy. 'You, on the other hand, kiss, as you do everything else: arrogantly!'

'But not savagely, right?' he suggested drily, and she gave him an aggravated look.

'Why did you do it?' she asked, shaking her head. 'You must have known I didn't expect you to.'

'What?' Morgan arched a dark brow. 'Kiss you?' He lifted his shoulders. 'I wanted to.'

'No.' Catherine could almost swear he had deliberately misunderstood her. 'Come here, to the office, to meet me.' She frowned. 'How did you find out where I worked anyway? Oh—not Denzil, please!'

'I did find out where you worked from him,' declared Morgan, taking her arm to guide her over the road, and although she gave him a horrified look, he was undeterred.

'I thought I made it clear——'

'I didn't precisely ask him where *you* worked,' he declared, allowing her to escape him again when they reached the opposite pavement. 'I asked where Kay worked, that's all.' He gave her a wry smile. 'Clever, hmm?'

Catherine expelled the breath she had hardly known she had been holding. 'Hardly,' she retorted, tersely. 'As Melvin, and at least half the other members of the staff, saw us together, it's not going to be long before it reaches Kay's ears, is it?'

Morgan gave her a sideways glance. 'And that matters to you.'

Catherine made a helpless gesture. 'It should matter to you.'

'Why?'

'Oh—well, because——'

'Because, what?'

'Well, because—Denzil's bound to find out, too.'

'So?'

'Oh . . .' Catherine felt herself flushing now. 'Don't be so obtuse. Denzil's bound to rag you about seeing me.' And that was an understatement, she thought bitterly.

Morgan's brows drew together. 'You and Denzil—is there something between you two?'

'You have to be joking!' Catherine was appalled.

'Do I?' Morgan didn't look convinced.

'Yes!' Catherine ground her teeth together. 'I know he's your cousin, but I wouldn't touch Denzil Sawyer with a barge-pole!'

Morgan's hand on her arm halted her abruptly. 'How do you know he's my cousin?' he demanded, and now there was no trace of warmth in his expression. 'What have they been saying?'

Catherine swallowed. 'Nothing. They've been saying nothing. Kay mentioned it, that's all. By accident, I think. The morning after the dinner party.'

'Ah . . .' He let her go then, and they continued walking towards the Embankment. Away to their left, the solid walls of the Tower of London rose against a clear blue sky, with the grey waters of the river reflecting their endurance. 'So—why wouldn't you touch old Denny with—what was it you said—a barge post?'

'A barge-pole,' corrected Catherine shortly, wishing they could get off this topic. 'I . . . just don't like him, that's all. I never did.'

'Never did,' echoed Morgan doggedly. 'That implies you've known him a long time.'

'Long enough.' Catherine hesitated. 'We—that is, Neil, my ex-husband, and I, used to go out with the Sawyers, in the old days. Since—since the divorce, I don't see much of them at all.'

'And that's a plus?'

'So far as Denzil is concerned, definitely.'

Morgan considered her averted face with some shrewdness. 'I guess he made a pass at you. Am I right?'

Catherine sighed. 'Yes. No——' She broke off, un-willing to say anything that might later be used to hurt Kay. 'That is—I'm not your cousin's type, believe me!'

'Why do you continually put yourself down?' Morgan protested, shaking his head. 'You've got beautiful skin, beautiful hair, beautiful eyes—even if you do have to wear these,' he added, pushing her spectacles up her nose with a careless finger. He gave her a crooked smile, his eyes sweeping intimately over her body. 'And a figure any man would kill to get his hands on!'

Catherine's face was burning now. 'Please,' she said, wishing the ground would simply open up and swallow her. 'You're embarrassing me.'

'Why? It's the truth.'

'It's not the truth.' Swallowing her pride, Catherine turned to look at him. 'I'm too tall, too fat and too ordinary to warrant compliments of that kind, and—and I wish you wouldn't make fun of me!'

Morgan's eyes narrowed. 'I guess this guy—what was his name? Neil? Yeah, Neil. I guess he's responsible for this low opinion you have of yourself, isn't he?'

'No——'

'Well, someone sure as hell is,' he ground out angrily. 'Lord, what do I have to do to make you believe me? I'm here, aren't I?'

'Only because I didn't fall into your arms at the first opportunity,' retorted Catherine, glad of the chance to tell him what she really thought. 'It must have been quite a novelty for you to find a woman who wasn't interested in your body! I dare say you thought that was why I took you home to dry off that night. Well, it wasn't. I felt sorry for you, that's all!'

There was silence after this outburst, and, glancing sideways at his closed, unreadable expression, Catherine felt a renewed sense of guilt. He hadn't, in all honesty, done anything to deserve the things she had said to him. She didn't really know why she had said what she did.

In effect, it had been a defensive gesture; a desire to defend herself, before any attack was imminent.

He halted suddenly, and Catherine, who had been unprepared for this move, walked on a few steps, before realising he wasn't with her. When she did comprehend what had happened, she looked behind her, and, seeing him just standing there, his hands in his pockets, she cautiously walked back.

'Morgan——'

Her use of his name was questioning, and he looked at her with eyes like yellow ice. 'That's me.'

Catherine licked her lips. 'I—what are you doing?' She lifted her shoulders awkwardly. 'I—thought we were going for a walk.'

Morgan's lips twisted. 'What's the point? As you said, I'm only interested in what you can do for me. If you're not prepared to come across, why should I waste my time with a homely broad like you?'

Catherine's colour drained away. No one, not even Neil at his cruellest, had ever made her feel so stupid— or so *ugly*. She felt shocked: beaten; totally defeated— and numbed by a pain that was threatening to tear her in two.

Her legs felt numb, too. When she tried to move them, they felt like two amorphous lumps of jelly that wouldn't go where she wanted them. She wanted to run. She wanted to put as much distance between her and Morgan Lynch as was humanly possible, but all she could do was stumble away. And, when she heard the footsteps coming after her, there was nothing she could do. He caught her easily, effortlessly overpowering her feeble attempts to fight him off, and propelling her back to where he had been standing before. That was when she saw the car. The sleek grey Mercedes was parked at the kerb, right where he had halted. And, although she did her best to resist him, he bundled her inside, sliding in after her, so that she was forced to scramble inelegantly over the gear console.

She heard him lock the door behind him, long before she could reach the passenger door-handle. It had a central locking system, of course, so there was no point in her thinking she could escape that way. She was trapped in here with him, for as long as he chose to detain her. Unless she hammered on the windows, she thought bitterly. And did she really want to draw attention to herself all over again?

'I'm sorry.'

The harsh apology took Catherine completely by surprise. She had been endeavouring to pull the skirt of her coat down around her knees. Her unconventional entry into the car had left her clothes in some confusion, her blouse having separated from her waistband, and her skirt riding up around her thighs. However, when Morgan spoke, her hands momentarily stilled, her eyes moving to his dark face, as disbelief warred with uncertainty.

'I mean it,' he said, half turning towards her, his left arm dropping along the seat behind her. She felt his fingers brush her hair, and jerked her head away, but his hand still descended on her nape. 'You've only yourself to blame,' he continued, the pad of his thumb massaging a spot just below her ear. 'Christ, how do you think I feel, when you accuse me of lying about you, just to get you into bed? That is how you think I get my kicks, isn't it? The things I've said about you—they're just a come-on, right?'

'Well, aren't they?'

Catherine turned her head and looked at him, trying not to show how his caressing fingers were affecting her. This was all a game to him, she was still convinced of that. It had to be. Men like him were not interested in— how was it he had put it? In 'homely broads' like her!

'No,' Morgan retorted now, startling her. His eyes darkened. 'At least—not for the reasons you say,' he added, his gaze dropping to where the buttons of her blouse had parted in their struggle to reveal the lacy bra beneath. 'I want to go to bed with you. I'd be a fool if I didn't. But not to satisfy some belief I have that I'm irresistible to women! I'm not. You've proved that, haven't you? I'm just a regular guy, who finds you very attractive. What's so unusual about that, for God's sake?'

Catherine bent her head. 'Why?'

'Why what?'

'Why me?' She took an uneven breath. 'Did—did Denzil put you up to it?'

Morgan swore softly, and then, as if unable to prevent himself, he bent towards her, his mouth covering hers with uncontrolled intent.

Catherine strained away from him, but the door at her back was an unyielding barrier. There was no escape within the limited confines of the car, and the hand she pressed against his chest was no deterrent to his determination. His weight compelled her back against the seat and when breathlessness decreed that she take a gulp of air, his tongue slipped between her teeth.

Immediately, the whole tenor of their embrace changed. The heated pressure of his lips gave way to a hot, wet invasion, his tongue stroking hers like rough velvet. Her spectacles misted over, and, as if he objected to not being able to look into her eyes, they were discarded on to the dashboard. Then his free hand gripped her thigh just above her knee, and the passing thought— that she had obviously not succeeded in pulling down her skirt—was quickly stifled by the hungry urgency of his kiss.

Her senses were swimming with the mindless passion he was evoking, and she couldn't prevent her hands from sliding into the thick dark hair at the back of his neck.

His hair was so clean, and smooth, and silky, clinging to her fingers when she wound the rich strands around them, and he made a strangled sound in his throat, his hand moving further up her leg.

And then, abruptly, she was free, and Morgan was moving back into his own seat, straightening his trousers, and adjusting the lapels of his jacket. Running one hand over his crotch, and the other through the tumbled state of his hair, he made a concerted effort to control himself, and Catherine took the opportunity to button her blouse. But her fingers trembled as she endeavoured to thread the buttons back into the holes, and Morgan, noticing her difficulty, brushed her hands aside.

'I'll do it,' he said huskily, taking hold of the offending studs, and, although she resented his high-handedness, she let him take over. The unusual awareness of her own arousal, that was heightened when his knuckles brushed the sensitive skin above her breasts, was causing her no small sense of anxiety. And, while she realised she should be grateful to him for calling a halt to something that had rapidly been getting out of hand, she wished she had been the one to do it.

'There you are,' he said, after a moment, tugging the two sides of her coat across her chest, as if he couldn't bear to look at what he'd done. 'And here are your glasses,' he added, rescuing them from the ledge in front of him. He watched her put them on, and then slumped down in his seat. 'OK.'

Catherine's tongue appeared to moisten her lips. 'Can I go now?'

'If you want to.' Morgan was staring straight ahead, and she saw to her relief that no one outside the car seemed to have noticed what was going on inside it.

'Well—if you'll unlock the door——'

'Don't you want lunch?' he interrupted her shortly, and her eyes widened with the incongruity of his question.

'Lunch?' she repeated, staring at him, in what she hoped was cold disbelief. 'Do you realise what time...? *Oh, God*!'

Her scathing question gave way to real dismay, and he looked at her. But Catherine was staring at her watch, unable to believe what she was seeing. It was nearly two o'clock! She had been due back at the office about fifteen minutes ago, and here she was, at least ten minutes' walk from Cannon Square.

'What's wrong?'

His tawny eyes were concerned, and, forgetting for a moment that he had just forced her into the car against her will, and taken advantage of her, Catherine told him.

'So what?' he said carelessly. 'I'm late, too, but I doubt if the might of the US Embassy will grind to a halt because of it.'

Catherine gave him an impatient look. 'I don't suppose it matters to you——'

'I don't suppose it does.'

'But I'm never late.'

'There's always a first time.'

Morgan's response was mocking, and, guessing she was going to get no help from him, Catherine reached to open the door.

'Wait.' His voice arrested her. 'I'll take you back, you know that. But—well, as you're late already, it wouldn't hurt to compound the offence, would it?'

'If you think I'm going to some restaurant——'

'Who said anything about a restaurant?' With a wry grimace Morgan turned, and hauled a small picnic basket off the back seat. He balanced it on the console between them, and flicked it open. 'Sandwiches, fruit, and a bottle of champagne,' he said, looking up into her astonished face. 'It was supposed to be someplace more romantic than this.' He indicated the customs buildings across the street. 'But what the hell? It's better than nothing.'

Catherine shook her head. 'You planned all this.'

'Well—not all of it,' he admitted drily, his eyes holding hers with disconcerting solemnity. 'Particularly not all that garbage about why I'm seeing you.' He gave a short, mirthless laugh. 'I guess I really blew it, didn't I? Just now. God, I didn't mean to get so heavy! You going on about Denny bugged me, I guess.'

Catherine caught her lower lip between her teeth. 'I think—I think we should just forget about it,' she said, realising how prudish that sounded. She put a nervous hand up to her spectacles. 'Where did this come from?'

'The picnic?' Morgan shrugged. 'I bought it.' He paused. 'Are you going to have some?'

Catherine hesitated. 'Are you?'

'Sure.' Morgan was indifferent. 'I'm hungry. If I can't have what I really want, I guess eating's the next best thing.'

'Oh.'

Catherine bent her head, and he sighed. 'Have I shocked you?'

'Of course not.' She cupped her jaw with slightly unsteady fingers. 'You—you do deliberately try to shock me though, don't you?'

'It's not difficult,' he responded, lifting the bottle of Cristal and gently easing out the cork. It hissed enticingly, and he nodded towards the basket. 'Pick up the glasses, and I'll pour this stuff.'

The question as to whether or not Catherine would have lunch seemed to have been decided for her, but she didn't say anything. If she was totally honest, she would admit that Morgan's idea of having a picnic appealed to her, and, ignoring the dictates of her conscience, she raised her glass to her lips.

The champagne was cool and sparkling, with an effervescence that went straight to her head. Catherine had always been ambivalent where champagne was concerned, but she realised now that that was because she

had never tasted the real thing. The champagne she and
Neil had had at their wedding, and which was brought
out at office parties, was nothing like this. This was deliciously light, and unknowingly potent, tickling her
palate, and loosening her tongue.

Munching on a delicately thin smoked salmon
sandwich, she felt more relaxed than she had ever done
in his presence, and, taking another sip of her champagne, she looked at him over the rim of her glass. 'Why
did the Sawyers ask you to dinner?' she queried, asking
the question she had been wanting to ask ever since that
evening, and Morgan considered the wine in his glass
before replying.

'I—guess because I've only been in England a month,'
he said at last. 'Have another sandwich.'

'I shouldn't.'

Catherine pulled a rueful face, and Morgan arched an
enquiring brow. 'Why not?'

'Oh—well, because I shouldn't,' she declared. 'I
should be losing weight, not trying to put it on.'

'You're not fat.' Morgan's gaze would have disturbed
her at any other time. 'You're not thin, but you're not
fat.'

Catherine grimaced. 'Overweight, then.'

'I wouldn't say so.' Morgan's mouth twisted. 'Don't
be so self-conscious. I like you just the way you are.'

'But not enough to——'

Catherine broke off in confusion, pressing a hand to
her mouth as if to silence her runaway tongue, and
Morgan's eyes darkened.

'Not enough for what?' he asked, holding her gaze,
and she felt the heat rising up from her neck.

'Nothing. It doesn't matter,' she said, dragging her
gaze away to look at the sandwich her fingers were
tearing apart.

'Not enough to—try and make it?' he suggested softly,
and the look she darted at him over the tops of her spec-

tacles was answer enough. 'Hey, I haven't made it in a car since I was sixteen!'

Sixteen! Catherine swallowed. When she had been sixteen, she had been more concerned with books than boys. The kind of girls who preferred the latter were not the kind of girls her mother had wanted her to associate with, but she could quite believe Morgan would have had no such qualms. On the contrary, if he had looked anything like he looked now at sixteen—and he must have done—she doubted the girls would have given him much choice in the matter.

She shook her head, and Morgan expelled a heavy breath. 'You think I didn't want to?' he demanded, his voice low and harsh, and she realised she was getting out of her depth.

'It doesn't matter,' she said again, putting down her glass, as the association between her careless words and the heady brew she was drinking coalesced. 'Er—how long have you worked for—for the Embassy?'

'A month.'

Catherine's brows drew together. 'The—month you've been in England.'

'Right.'

Catherine hesitated. It was obvious he didn't want to talk about himself, but anything was better than risking another indiscretion, and swallowing another mouthful of her sandwich, she said, 'And—before that?'

Morgan's mouth compressed. 'Washington.'

'You worked at the Pentagon?'

'No. Not at the Pentagon.'

Ignoring his increasingly withdrawn expression, Catherine forced herself to go on. 'Denzil worked at the Pentagon, before he came to London,' she said.

'Did he?' Morgan didn't sound interested.

'Yes.' Catherine considered for a moment, and then took another sip of her champagne to fortify her. 'And— you and he were old army buddies, weren't you?'

Morgan picked up the champagne bottle. 'Who told you that?'

Catherine licked her lips. 'Didn't you?'

'No.' He was very definite about that.

'Oh—well, then, Kay must have done,' she declared carelessly. 'Does it matter? You were in the army, weren't you?' Another thought occurred to her. 'Did they show you how to do what you did to Melvin?'

Morgan was scowling now, and she knew she was treading the very thin line between advantage and disaster. 'What did they teach you? Karate?'

Morgan gave her another daunting look, and then thrust the bottle back into the basket. 'I guess,' he answered curtly, and, when she refused anything else to eat, he tossed the wicker basket on to the back seat of the Mercedes. She wasn't sure, but she suspected the bottle wasn't empty, and the possibility that he had spilled champagne over the glove-soft leather upholstery caused her head to turn. But she sensed anything she said now would be futile, and she was not surprised when he leant forward and started the engine.

'I guess you'd better buckle up,' he said, checking the rear-view mirror for traffic, and, before she could empty her glass, they were moving away.

It was half-past two when he dropped her outside the block of offices, pausing only long enough for her to make a hasty exit from the car.

'Thank you for lunch,' she said awkwardly, but Morgan only nodded, before setting the tyres spinning. The Mercedes disappeared around the corner of Cannon Square without him giving her so much as a backward glance, and Catherine entered the building with a distinct sense of anticlimax. Not even the lingering taste of the champagne could elevate her mood, and she made her way to her desk feeling totally deflated.

*   *   *

'Are you all right?'

She had hardly settled into her seat before Melvin Scott
was beside her, and, looking up into his flushed, anxious
face, she stifled her own miseries.

'Of course,' she said, as if it was the most natural
thing in the world for a strange man—a strange man to
her colleagues, at least—to accost her in the street.
'Surely you weren't worried about me?'

'Well, of course I was worried,' exclaimed Melvin
tersely. 'Do you know what time it is?'

'I know.' Catherine tried to keep the edge out of her
voice without really succeeding. 'I—er—well, you know
what—restaurants are like. They take ages to serve you.'

Melvin frowned. 'That's where you've been? Having
lunch in some restaurant?'

'Where else?' Catherine wondered at her own capacity
for lying. 'I'm sorry if you thought something terrible
had happened to me, but, as you can see, I'm still in
one piece.'

'Hmm,' Melvin acknowleged the truth of this
statement, but he still looked troubled. 'You—er—you've
known him some time, huh?'

Catherine sighed. 'Does it matter?'

'No. No, I suppose not.' Melvin looked a little sulky
now. 'But I'd look out for myself, if I were you. He can
be a nasty customer, when it suits him.'

Catherine bit her lip. 'I'm sorry if he hurt you,
Mel——'

'Oh, that's nothing.' Melvin dismissed her apology
with some indignation. 'He didn't *hurt* me. Well—not
really. But you wouldn't stand much chance with him,
if he turned awkward.'

'I realise that.' Catherine was getting tired of this conversation. Besides, Melvin's voice was carrying right
round the room, and she doubted any of her fellow op-
erators was in any doubt as to how she had spent her
lunch hour.

'Anyway, if you're sure you know what you're doing...'

'I do.' Catherine was terse now.

'Well—all right. Oh—by the way...'

'Yes?'

'John was looking for you earlier. He wanted some figures you were supposed to have ready for him.'

'Oh, yes.' It was a salutory reminder of what she was supposed to be thinking about. 'I'll—er—I'll get them printed right away. Thanks, Melvin.' She paused, and then added reluctantly, 'For everything.'

CHAPTER SEVEN

CATHERINE spent the rest of the day anticipating Kay's appearance, but Mr Hollingsworth must have kept her busy, because her friend did not come around. And, in spite of her prolonged lunch hour, John Humphries made no complaint. 'It's not as if it happens every day,' he remarked, after complimenting her on the set of figures she had given him. 'Who is this chap? Anyone I know?'

'I don't think so,' said Catherine politely, loading some papers she wanted to take home into her briefcase. 'Thanks, John. See you in the morning.'

She thought he would have liked to have continued with the discussion, but Catherine had had enough for one day. There was still the corridor, and the lift, to face, and she was overwhelmingly relieved when she emerged from the building without having to give another account of herself. Really, she thought, men could be as bad as women sometimes. Melvin had acted just as her mother would have done, and even John Humphries had shown he was not indifferent to her activities. She was supposed to be free, and unattached. Yet as soon as another man came on the scene, everyone wanted to get in on the act.

Only Hector asked no questions, she reminded herself, later that evening, tucked up on her armchair, in front of the television. At least he took her as he found her, making no statements, no generalisations, and definitely no criticisms. Ensconced on her lap, he was quite content to share her space, but never overrun it. They each had their own place, she told herself firmly, and then wondered why that declaration suddenly seemed so hollow.

Damn Morgan Lynch, she thought painfully, sniffing. It was all his fault. Before he had come on the scene, her life had been so uncomplicated. Oh, she had been nursing a misapprehension about her feelings for Neil, but that hadn't really been important. In fact, it had probably helped her to be more discerning when it came to other relationships.

But with Morgan there had been no discernment, no choice, just a blind need that grew with every minute she spent in his company. And it was so crazy! She had never been that kind of girl. She had always considered sex as a vastly overrated pastime, and her relationship with Neil had owed more to a simple compatibility with one another than to any great passion on either side. Indeed, she had been firmly convinced she was incapable of feelings of that kind, and it had come as no real surprise to discover that she couldn't have children. It had hurt, of course. No woman liked to feel she was incapable of accomplishing her primary role in life, but her work had always been ample compensation. Now it wasn't. Now she found herself wanting other things, and the very idea of having a baby with Morgan filled her with emotions that were insanely distracting.

Her lips tightened. Not that her deficiency was likely to mean anything to him, she thought bitterly. Morgan was firmly in control of his feelings where she was concerned, and, although he apparently felt some attraction for her, there were limitations on their relationship. It was all right as long as she understood what those limitations were, but if she overstepped some invisible line he had drawn the consequences were obvious.

Well, to hell with him, she thought tearfully, rubbing the heels of her hands across her eyes. If his fragile ego couldn't stand a few simple questions it was just too bad. The next time—if there was a next time, she admitted tremulously—he came around, she would tell him to get lost. Her original fears about getting involved with him had been justified, and she might as well get out now, before he really hurt her.

She had gone into the kitchen to make herself a cup of cocoa when the doorbell rang. Hector miaowed, and Catherine stood, with a saucepan of milk clutched in one hand and a teaspoon in the other, momentarily incapable of thought. Then, setting the saucepan down, she took the breath she had been holding. Morgan, she guessed, running nervous hands down the seams of her sweat pants. He must have had second thoughts after leaving her that afternoon, and come back to apologise. And here she was, looking her worst in the outfit she used to do her aerobics.

But, so what? she asked herself abruptly. Good heavens, only five minutes ago she had been rehearsing what she would say if he came around again, and she was getting into a panic, just because she didn't look her best. What did it matter? She wasn't going to let him in. *Was she...?*

Even so, as she walked along the hall, she couldn't help noticing how the long-sleeved leotard hugged her full breasts, and how the loose-fitting pants exaggerated the swell of her hips. If only she had had her bath, as she had intended. But she had flopped down into her chair after exercising, and apathy had kept her there, staring mindlessly at the television. But it was too late now, and, summoning all her confidence, she pulled open the door.

'Neil!'

Never in her wildest dreams had she expected to find her ex-husband on her doorstep. Since the divorce, she had seen him only once and then in company with her solicitor. There had been no social contact whatsoever, and for a moment the sense of devastation that gripped her at the realisation that it wasn't Morgan robbed her face of all colour.

'Catherine.' Neil acknowledged her stunned use of his name with some concern. Then, misinterpreting her reaction, he added gently, 'I'm sorry if I frightened you.'

'You didn't.' Catherine struggled to regain her composure. She might have had doubts about her ability to handle Morgan, but she had none where her ex-husband was concerned. 'What do you want, Neil?'

'Can I come in?'

'Come in?' She was staggered, and showed it. She looked beyond him. 'Is—er—is Marie with you?'

'No. I'm alone.' Neil checked his tie with what she recognised was a nervous hand. 'I—can we talk?'

Catherine shook her head, but after a moment she stepped aside to allow him into the house. How could she refuse? she thought resignedly. They were not enemies, after all. In fact, they had had an amazingly civilised divorce, and, although it had been due in no small part to her desire for anonymity, Neil had been co-operative when she had wanted to keep the house.

'Oh—this is nice,' he said now, walking into the sitting-room, and Catherine thought how amazing it was that his presence in the room meant absolutely nothing to her. He could have been a stranger, and, treating him as she would a stranger, she offered him a seat.

'I was just making some co—coffee,' she said, changing the word at the last minute. What little pride she had would not admit to making cocoa. It smacked of hot water bottles, and bed-jackets, and she had no intention of providing him with that kind of ammunition.

'I'd prefer something stronger, if you have it,' Neil answered now, perching on the edge of the sofa. 'But if not, coffee will do. It's damn cold out there.'

'Is it?' Catherine lifted her shoulders in an indifferent gesture.

'You'd better believe it.' Neil stretched his neck, as if his collar was too tight, and Catherine remembered how that particular habit of his used to irritate her.

Turning away, she ran a hand round the back of her neck, under the silky weight of her hair. 'I've got some sherry,' she said, opening the door of a darkwood cabinet. 'Will that do?'

'Fine.' Neil nodded. 'Will you join me?'

'I don't think so.' Catherine glanced thoughtfully towards the kitchen, and then, lifting Hector into her arms, she seated herself in her armchair again. 'I don't want anything right now.'

'Oh—well, OK.' Neil swallowed a generous mouthful of the oloroso she had given him, and licked his lips in appreciation. 'This is good.'

'Good.' Catherine pushed her spectacles up her nose, and regarded him coolly through the curved lenses. 'So, what do you want?'

Neil grimaced. 'That's not very friendly. Why do I have to *want* something? Perhaps this is just a social call.'

'Neil——'

'Well, it could be. We are still friends, aren't we?' He looked down at his drink. 'I thought we were.'

Catherine sighed. 'Neil,' she said again, and he looked up at her with curiously defensive eyes.

'You're looking well, anyway,' he said, and for once she didn't wilt beneath his critical appraisal. 'Really well,' he added. 'You always were a good-looking woman.'

Catherine almost gasped. 'You didn't used to think so.'

'Yes, I did.' Neil was indignant. 'Oh, I know I've said some cruel things in my time, but I didn't always mean them. Haven't you ever said anything in the heat of the moment, and then regretted it later?'

Catherine stared at him in disbelief. 'You're not telling me you came round here just to see how I am?'

Neil pulled a wry face. 'Not exactly.'

'What then?'

He sighed now, and stretched his neck again. 'I—er—I ran into Mrs Scott yesterday,' he said, with some diffidence. 'You know the Scotts, don't you? They live——'

'Across the street. Yes, I know who they are,' Catherine agreed shortly. 'So?'

Neil cradled his glass between his hands, and hunched his shoulders. 'You're not making this easy for me, Catherine,' he muttered, casting a resentful look at Hector, curled so confidingly in her lap. 'I only have your best interests at heart, you know that. Why do you have to make me feel as if I'm being nosy?'

'Are you being nosy, Neil?' Catherine was beginning to get an inkling of what this might be about. 'What did Mrs Scott tell you? I imagine she must have told you something, or you wouldn't have brought her name up.'

For a moment, his anger flared. 'You're so clever, aren't you?' he snapped. 'Always thought yourself cleverer than me. All right, so Mrs Scott did talk about you. Why shouldn't she voice her opinion? People round here are pretty conservative on the whole, and if you start letting men out of the house at six o'clock in the morning, what do you expect?'

Catherine was furious. 'And you came all the way from Cavendish Mews just to tell me this?'

'Not exactly.' Neil held up his head. 'Naturally, I was concerned——'

'Why?'

'Well, you were my wife——'

'*Were* being the operative word,' retorted Catherine, pushing an indignant Hector off her knee, and getting to her feet. 'How dare you think you can come here and make any remarks about what I do or don't do? My life is my own, Neil. And I'll do what I like with it.'

Neil's mouth took on a sullen twist, but he didn't get up. 'Well, who is he?' he demanded, looking up at her.

'Who?' Catherine put her hands on her hips and regarded him contemptuously. 'You said *men*, didn't you?'

Neil did get up then, emptying his glass and setting it down noisily on the coffee-table. 'Stop trying to provoke me,' he said. 'You know who I mean.'

'Do I?' Catherine found she was enjoying this in a funny, self-derisory kind of way.

'Yes.' Neil's mouth worked uncertainly. 'Is it someone I know? Not—Simon Lewis!'

'It's none of your business.' Catherine was adamant.

'Then it is him!'

'No, it's not.' Catherine was frustrated, but she refused to give him that satisfaction. Neil had always regarded Simon as a bit of a wimp, and it would have cheered his ego no end to think that Catherine had been compelled to resort to his company. 'It's no one you know, but that's as far as I'm prepared to go. Now—will you?'

'Will I what?'

'Go,' said Catherine pointedly. 'And mind your own business in future.'

Neil looked at her rather strangely now. 'I always thought you were my business,' he said, surprising her again. He bit his lip. 'I still love you, you know, Cat.'

Catherine caught her breath. 'No, you don't——'

'I do.' Neil's expression grew faintly resentful. 'If you hadn't been so all-fire keen to pursue your career, we'd probably still be together. A man only goes looking for what he can't find at home.'

'Oh, honestly!' Catherine stared at him. 'Is that the excuse you've invented?'

'It's not an excuse——'

'Well, it certainly sounds like one.' Catherine couldn't believe this was happening. 'I thought you were in love with Marie. At least, that's what you told me when you said you were leaving.'

Neil shrugged. 'I thought I did.'

'You *thought* you did!'

'Yes.' Neil made a defensive gesture. 'But—well, things haven't been too good between Marie and me lately, and then, when I saw Mrs Scott——'

'You thought you'd come and say your piece!'

'As I say, I still care about you, Cat——'

'Do you?' Once, that would have meant so much, but now it was only academic. 'Well, I'm sorry, Neil, but I don't care about you. Not any more.'

'I don't believe that——'

He grabbed her arm then, trying to pull her towards him, but Catherine fought him off. One of the advantages of being as tall as she was, she thought wryly, realising she wouldn't have escaped Morgan so easily. She suspected Neil's real motive was that he resented her becoming involved with anyone else. It was all right so long as he thought she was sitting at home, pining for him. Discovering she was making a life of her own must have really pricked his ego.

'It's the truth,' she said, when she was free of him, rubbing the arm he had held with rueful fingers. 'You can't rekindle something that's already dead and cold.'

Neil scowled. 'I suppose you think this man, whoever he is, will marry you,' he sneered. 'Getting a bit old to play the field, aren't you, Cat?'

This was more like the Neil she remembered, and Catherine sighed. 'Just go, Neil.'

'Oh, I will.' Neil moved aggressively towards the door, and Hector scurried out of his path. 'But don't forget what I've said. You may be riding high now but this bloke may not be so keen when you tell him you can't have children.'

Catherine closed her eyes as he passed her. Only Neil would have brought that up, she thought disgustedly.

Why hadn't she ever realised before how mean and small-minded he was?

Opening her eyes again, she picked up Hector, and followed Neil along the hall, noticing almost inconsequently how thin he was. Even the trousers of the suit he was wearing looked too baggy on him. Unwillingly she was reminded of Morgan's hips, and his buttocks, which were lean and tight beneath his jeans, but tautly muscled. Morgan's legs, too, were not like Neil's legs. They were muscled, as well; strong and powerful. Not like the legs of someone who worked in an office at all, she reflected, with sudden perception. Was that why his skin was so darkly tanned? she wondered. Because he was more used to working outdoors? Of course, it could be because he did a lot of sports, she argued. Watersports, or skiing; golf, even. One thing was for sure—he was unlikely to tell her.

'I'll go, then.' Neil had opened the door, and paused on the step. Catherine inclined her head.

'Goodbye,' she said, unconsciously stroking Hector's ears as she spoke, and Neil's lip curled.

'What's he?' he asked contemptuously. 'A substitute?' and Catherine slammed the door in his face, no longer able to hide her feelings.

Of course, she still had Kay to face, and Catherine was not surprised when the other girl appeared midway through the following morning. But, just as she was preparing to fend off the inevitable questions, Kay said, 'Are you free for lunch?'

Catherine blinked, and adjusted her spectacles. 'For lunch?' she echoed, surprised at the invitation. It was months since she and Kay had had lunch together, and, whenever they did, it was always planned days in advance.

'Yes. Today,' said Kay, glancing over her shoulder, and Catherine guessed she was taking Mr Hollingsworth's threats seriously. 'I have to talk to you.'

Inwardly, Catherine groaned. She could guess what about. Why couldn't people just allow her to get on with her life, in her own way? she wondered wearily. They meant well, she was sure. At least, some of them did. But she wasn't a child, after all. If she made mistakes, that was her prerogative.

Now, she shook her head. 'I—don't know, Kay. I am—pretty busy.'

'It's important,' said Kay flatly, and, realising she couldn't put it off indefinitely, Catherine gave in.

'Oh—all right,' she said, resting her elbows on the table and cupping the back of her neck with her hands. 'One o'clock, OK?'

'One o'clock,' agreed Kay, with none of her usual ebullience, and, watching her friend walk quickly across the floor and out of the office, Catherine surmised that she was in for another lecture. But why? she pondered wryly. Morgan *was* Denzil's cousin, and they had engineered the introduction. Surely the fact that Morgan had kissed her in full view of the accountancy department didn't warrant some kind of formal warning? They didn't know the half of it, for heaven's sake!

Still, Kay had always been fairly straight with her, and she supposed she did owe her an explanation. She just hoped she could get away without being too honest. There were things about her association with Morgan that she preferred to keep to herself.

They went to Salki's, a little Italian restaurant in the next street, where the pizzas tasted nothing like the pre-packed ones Catherine occasionally bought at the supermarket. She studied the menu with a jaundiced eye, aware that everything she liked was at least a thousand calories, and then rejected her misgivings. So what? she thought resignedly, choosing the deep-pan cheese and tomato, with extra cheese, for good measure. She might need this. Kay was looking awfully serious.

The waiter brought a pot of coffee for them to share while their pizzas were cooking, and Kay waited until Catherine had added cream and was stirring the fragrant brew before she said shortly, 'Why didn't you tell me you were seeing Morgan?'

Catherine gave herself a moment to absorb this, and then looked up. 'I'm not exactly—seeing him,' she admitted evenly. 'Not in the way you mean, anyway.'

Kay snorted. 'Don't give me that! Not after what happened yesterday.'

Catherine could feel a faint prickling of irritation. What gave Kay the right to speak to her like this? she wondered tightly. When had she ceased to function as an intelligent adult?

'What did happen yesterday?' she enquired, refusing to make it easy for her. 'Why don't you refresh my memory?'

Kay looked a little disconcerted now, but she ploughed on. 'I never thought you could be so—so irresponsible!' she declared tersely. 'It's not as if you don't know what kind of man he is!'

Catherine expelled her breath carefully. 'What kind of man is he?' she demanded. 'You tell me.'

Kay ran distracted fingers into her mop of blonde curls. 'I always thought you were so sensible,' she said, evading the question. 'When Denzil suggested you should join us for dinner, I was sure it would be all right. I mean,' she spread an expressive hand, 'you said yourself, you didn't want to get involved—with anyone.'

Catherine caught her lower lip between her teeth. 'Does it matter?' She paused. 'What *is* wrong?' A cold hand gripped her heart. 'He's not really married, is he?'

'No!' Kay's dismissal of the idea was so derisory that Catherine was forced to believe her. 'I told you. He was married—once. But that was over before—well, years ago anyway,' she finished hastily.

Catherine shook her head. 'So? Why all this?' She indicated the restaurant. 'I can't believe you brought me here just to express your disapproval.'

'I didn't.' Kay gave her a resentful look. 'Honestly, Cat, I thought you had more sense!'

Catherine felt a twinge of perception. 'Don't you mean, you expected Morgan would have?' she suggested drily.

'What do you mean?' Kay's face turned red, and, re-alising she had struck a nerve, Catherine pressed on.

'I mean, you didn't think Morgan would be interested in someone like me, did you?' she asked equably. 'As you said, he is a very attractive man. Why would he go for someone who couldn't even keep her own husband?'

'It's not like that!' Kay looked indignant now, but Catherine suspected there was a grain of truth there, somewhere. 'I've never blamed you for Neil walking out.'

'Denzil does.'

'Yes—well, Denzil likes Neil. They're a lot alike.'

More than you know, thought Catherine drily, but she merely acknowledged her friend's words with an indifferent lift of her shoulders.

'Anyway, that doesn't alter the fact that your getting involved with Morgan Lynch is—not a good idea.'

Catherine was pretty sure Kay would have preferred to use a stronger expletive, but experience had taught her caution, too. Waiting until the waiter had set their pizzas down in front of them, she went on in the same conciliatory vein. 'You don't understand, you see,' she said, taking out her frustration on the pizza, 'Morgan was in Vietnam.'

'Was he?'

Catherine barely whispered the words, but, before she had had the chance to consider the implications of this revelation, Kay continued.

'He volunteered, you see. He didn't have to go, of course. Denzil never did. And with Morgan's father—well, never mind about that now. Suffice it to say that Morgan has never done what his family expected of him.'

Catherine frowned. 'But what has that to do with my seeing him? I'm not,' she added swiftly. 'But—if I were.'

'Oh!' Kay sighed. 'Must I spell it out for you? You know what happened to men in Vietnam!'

'I believe it was pretty horrific.'

'There was nothing *pretty* about it,' retorted Kay grimly, and Catherine inclined her head.

'All right. Perhaps that was the wrong word to use. I assume you're saying he saw active service.'

'He *enlisted*, Cat. Of course he saw active service.'

Catherine sighed. 'Well, I'm sorry if I seem obtuse, but I still don't see what you're getting at.'

'He was captured, Cat. By the Vietcong. They *tortured* him!'

The smell of the pizza was suddenly more than Catherine could stomach. Pushing her plate aside, she poured herself another cup of coffee, hoping Kay wouldn't notice that her hands were trembling.

'Now do you see what I'm getting at?' Kay demanded, apparently as indifferent to the food as her friend. Having mangled her pizza, she too pushed the plate aside, and propping her elbow on the table, she rested her head on her hand. 'When he came home, he spent at least two years in a mental institution!'

Catherine felt sick. Physically sick. All around them, the sounds of the restaurant were going on. Plates clattering, cutlery jangling, the steady hum of conversation from the patrons. But all she could hear was the keening sound Morgan had made that night he'd slept on her sofa, and all she could see was his sweat-streaked face, as he'd apologised for waking her up.

'Are you OK?'

Kay was looking at her oddly now, and, realising she couldn't allow the other girl to know what she was thinking, Catherine managed to nod her head.

'Yes, fine,' she lied, even though she had never been so close to throwing up. 'Er—could we get out of here, do you think? I'm not very hungry after all.'

'Nor am I,' admitted Kay, summoning the waiter with evident relief.

Outside, the cool damp air was reviving. Catherine could feel the nausea receding, and the colour came back into her face. The Vietnam war had been over for fifteen years, she reminded herself. There was no way those sadistic monsters could hurt him now.

'So you see, don't you,' said Kay, continuing her argument, as they walked back to the office, 'it's crazy for you to get involved with someone like him. Oh, I know he's Denzil's cousin—*second* cousin,' she amended, as if it was important to emphasise that remove, 'but Denzil only acknowledges their relationship because he has to.'

'He has to?' echoed Catherine, still busy with her own thoughts, but catching those words, and Kay sighed.

'Well, you might as well know, I suppose,' she said shortly. 'Denzil will probably kill me when I tell him I've told you, but Morgan's father is General Lynch. He's virtually retired now, but he was one of the security advisers at the Pentagon.'

'I see.'

The pieces were beginning to fall into place. That was no doubt why the Sawyers had been obliged to invite Morgan to dinner. As he was General Lynch's son, Denzil couldn't afford to offend him. Not overtly, anyway, she appended, remembering how the two men had almost come to blows.

'Anyway, I'm glad we've had this talk,' Kay said, as they reached the swing doors of the office building. 'I mean, we have been friends for a lot of years, haven't we? And I couldn't let you go on thinking Denzil was to blame for what happened the other night.'

'Kay——'

'No. Let me finish. Morgan Lynch is poison, believe me. Actually, Denzil thinks he's still half-crazy; him, and that man who looks after him, both. His father should have left him down in Florida. He seemed happy enough there. But, no, General Alexander Lynch had to have his son doing something for his country, even if Morgan himself has no interest in the work.'

'At the Embassy?'

'At the Embassy,' agreed Kay, preceding Catherine into the lift. They were alone, and, pressing the button for the fourteenth floor, she gave the other woman a penetrating look. 'You do agree, don't you? You do see that there is absolutely no sense in going any further with the relationship?'

Catherine forced a tight smile. 'I've told you,' she said, 'we're not having a—relationship. We had—lunch together. That's all.'

Kay looked sceptical. 'But you did let him kiss you——'

'Well? Insanity's not contagious, is it?' enquired Catherine politely, and Kay gave her a doubtful look.

'You're not—I mean—you wouldn't…see him again, would you?' she ventured, clearly troubled by her friend's ambivalence, and Catherine was glad when the lift doors opened at the fourteenth floor and she could get out.

'Tell Denzil I appreciate his concern,' she replied, without really answering. 'Oh, look, is that Mr Hollingsworth looking for you?'

By the time Kay had realised this was just a diversion, Catherine had put at least a dozen yards between them.

And, as her office lay in precisely the opposite direction, she could hardly follow.

'I'll see you tomorrow,' she called, as Catherine disappeared around the corner, and Catherine was relieved to avoid any rejoinder.

CHAPTER EIGHT

A WEEK later, Catherine was forced to face the painful fact that she was unlikely to see Morgan again. He hadn't phoned; he hadn't called; she had had no communication with him whatsoever. Even the flowers he had sent the previous week were already losing their petals, and, although she knew she should throw them out, she had put off doing so. It was stupid really, but they had become her only remaining link with him, and, despite the fact that he had never touched them, they were the only tangible reality.

Of course, it had made things easier at Bracknells. She could tell Kay honestly that she was not seeing Morgan, and, without his disruptive influence on her life, she was able to put all her energies into her work. She suspected some of her appraisals were not as shrewd as she would have liked them to be, and the judgements she made weren't always verified by their performance. But she plodded on regardless, determined not to give in to her emotions.

After all, it wasn't as if they had had a real relationship, she told herself when she felt really down. At best, it had been a one-sided affair, with her being completely frank about her divorce—well, almost, she amended—and Morgan clamming up every time she asked a personal question. If she thought she knew now at least part of the reason why he had been so reticent, that didn't really change anything. It simply reinforced the fact that she hadn't known him—not the *real* Morgan Lynch, at any rate. All she had been permitted to see was the face

he showed to the rest of the world, the guarded mask
that hid so many secrets.

Except that night, she consoled herself in moments of
extreme adversity. Then, briefly, she had glimpsed what
those tortured memories were doing to his subconscious. She tried not to think about what his captors
might have done to him. She didn't want to think of him
starving, or filthy, or forced to suffer the basest kinds
of humiliation. She didn't want to think of him in *pain*.
It was as simple as that.

But that didn't stop the recollections of news items
she'd seen, articles she'd read, from filling her head with
horrific details. It seemed as if she couldn't open a newspaper or a magazine without reading some new report
of the atrocities that had been committed—not just
against the soldiers themselves, but against innocent civ-
ilians, caught up in the fighting. There were accusations
about the use of napalm, a form of jellied petrol, which
stuck and set fire to anything it touched; about the fact
that some soldiers developed a drug habit; and the un-
derlying problem of psychological difficulties. But when
she considered that the average age of the men fighting
in Vietnam was nineteen, Catherine didn't find that at
all surprising. Dear God, she thought, it was like sending
an army of college students to fight a war, and then being
shocked because they reacted against its futility.

The conversation she had had with Kay had satisfied
the doubts she had had about Morgan's not being used
to working in an office. Although Kay hadn't elaborated
about his being in Florida, Catherine suspected he had
spent a lot of his time there outdoors. It would explain
his physical appearance, and the fact that he had so little
interest in his present occupation. She wondered what
he had done in Florida. Whatever it was, he had been
happier then, she was sure of it. So why had his father
insisted on him returning to Washington? For that was

one thing Morgan had told her: he had worked in
Washington, before he had come to London.

But the things she did know about him seemed so insignificant compared to what she wanted to know. In
truth, she would have liked to know everything about
him, and, although she knew it was crazy, she couldn't
stop thinking about him.

So much for her determination not to get involved,
she thought ruefully as she prepared Hector's meal one
evening, about two weeks after the Sawyers' dinner party.
She should have stuck to her guns and refused their invitation. That way, she would never have met Morgan
Lynch.

The doorbell rang as she was running her bath.
Turning off the taps, Catherine went to answer it. As
luck would have it, she hadn't yet undressed, and only
the unbuttoned sleeves of her blouse flapped about her
wrists as she opened the door.

She didn't expect it to be Morgan, and it wasn't. In
the early days after their parting, she had jumped every
time the phone rang, and rushed to the door every time
she had a visitor. But she had long since admitted that
he wasn't going to contact her, so that finding her mother
on the doorstep was no great disappointment.

'Hello, darling.' Mrs Lambert kissed the air beside
Catherine's ear and stepped past her into the hall. 'Am
I intruding? Or do you have the time to offer me a cup
of tea?'

Catherine sighed, and closed the door. 'You're not
intruding,' she averred, gesturing for her mother to go
ahead. 'I was just going to have a bath, that's all.'

'Oh, well.' Mrs Lambert tucked the parcel she was
carrying under her arm, and preceded her daughter into
the kitchen. 'We can share a pot of tea then, can't we?'

'Why not?'

Catherine tried to sound enthusiastic, but she was unhappily aware that it didn't come out that way, and her

mother gave her a thoughtful look before noticing Hector, hunched over his feeding bowl.

'I see that creature still warrants primary attention,' she remarked, as Hector paused to give her a slant-eyed stare. 'Oh, get on with your fish-heads, or whatever it is you're eating! Don't look at me as if I had no right to be here.'

'Stop exaggerating, Mother,' exclaimed Catherine, going to fill the kettle. 'And sit down, if you're going to stay in here. Hector won't bite you. He's just curious, that's all.'

'Hmm.' Mrs Lambert didn't sound convinced, but she seated herself on one of the kitchen chairs, and put the parcel on the table beside her. Then, patting it, she said, 'You know what this is, of course.'

'I imagine it's the print,' replied Catherine, giving her a rueful look. 'I'm sorry. I forgot all about it.'

'Yes. I guessed you had.' Her mother nodded. 'I did wonder if you might come over last weekend, and every day this week I've expected you to phone, but of course, you haven't.'

Catherine finished setting out cups and saucers, and then, unable to delay any longer, she too sat down. 'It's been—pretty hectic, at work,' she murmured, not altogether untruthfully. 'I meant to phone, but——'

'But I come low on your list of priorities, is that it?' enquired Mrs Lambert drily. 'Yes, I had gathered that.'

Catherine shook her head. 'I'm sorry...'

'Well, that's something, I suppose.' Mrs Lambert pulled a wry face as her daughter busied herself opening the parcel. And then, perceptively, 'Is something wrong?'

'Wrong? What could be wrong?' asked Catherine defensively, pulling off the string, and unwrapping the brown paper. 'I'm fine—*oh*!'

She broke off as the print was revealed, swallowing convulsively. She had almost forgotten what it portrayed, but now, as she pushed the paper aside, the substance of the painting was exposed. She recalled then why she had liked it so much. The landscape at dusk, with its subtle hues of purple and blue and grey, was wonderfully evocative, just as she remembered. But what had caused her to take that sudden intake of breath was the distinctly oriental influence in the painting. The skyline, the fields, even the stark sinews of the bare trees, with the mountains beyond, were essentially Chinese in origin. Why had she never noticed it before? And why was she noticing it now?

Hot tears were suddenly pressing at the backs of her eyes, and, turning her face away, she dashed a hand across her cheek, almost dislodging her spectacles. 'Oh—the kettle's boiling,' she said, unutterably relieved to have an excuse to get up from the table. 'I'll make the tea.'

'I didn't realise you found it so moving,' remarked her mother, watching her daughter as she poured hot water into the teapot. 'I'll tell Fliss. She might know of other work the artist has done.'

'No...' Catherine answered too fast, and had to restrain herself. 'That is—one is enough for me. I—er—I haven't even decided where I'm going to put it.'

'How about your bedroom?' suggested Mrs Lambert shrewdly. 'Catherine...' She paused. 'Something is upsetting you, isn't it? Can't you talk about it?'

Catherine shook her head. 'There's nothing to talk about,' she denied. She glanced over her shoulder. 'Are—er—are you staying for a meal?'

'Are you inviting me?'

Catherine determinedly stirred the tea in the teapot. 'If you'd like to stay, you're welcome,' she said. 'It's only chicken salad.'

'Ah.' Her mother made a considering sound. 'You're slimming.'

'No.' Catherine turned to set the cups on the table. She could hardly tell her mother that her appetite had practically disappeared since Morgan had driven out of her life. 'It's simple to make, that's all.'

'Well, you have lost weight,' declared Mrs Lambert. 'And if you're not slimming, it must be something else. Have you seen your doctor?'

'Of course not.' Catherine set the teapot on its stand, and pushed both it and the jug towards her mother. 'Help yourself.'

Mrs Lambert poured her tea, added a splash of milk, and then sat back in her chair. 'Anyway,' she said, 'much as I would like to accept your somewhat...' she grimaced '...reluctant invitation, I can't. As a matter of fact, Billy brought me up to town. He'd arranged to have a drink with his broker at his club, so I suggested he dropped me here for an hour, and then I'd meet him for dinner later.'

'I see.'

It was a relief to know she wouldn't have to keep up an appearance of normality all evening, and Catherine was grateful. Billy Saunders was the latest in the long line of her mother's escorts, and, although she knew it was unlikely, their friendship did seem to be progressing into a genuine relationship.

'He's such a love,' said Mrs Lambert now, sipping her tea reflectively. 'He'll do anything for me, you know.' She looked at Catherine across her cup. 'It's a pity you don't know anyone like that, darling.'

'Yes, isn't it?' agreed Catherine shortly, looking down at her hand where it rested on the table. 'What time are you meeting him?'

'Seven o'clock,' replied her mother, with just the faintest edge to her voice. 'You don't have to look at your watch. I'll be going soon.'

'I wasn't.' Catherine was indignant, but when she lifted her head, and met her mother's penetrating stare, she realised that had just been a ploy to attract her attention.

'It's not Neil, is it?' Mrs Lambert ventured now. 'He hasn't been pestering you, has he?' She waited, and getting no answer, she went on, 'I did hear he and Marie were having problems, and it would be like him to try and shift them on to somebody else.'

Catherine moistened her lips. The reason she hadn't produced an immediate reply was simple enough. Sometimes, her mother's perspicacity amazed her, and she was wondering whether she should tell her about Neil's unsolicited visit when Mrs Lambert spoke again.

'You wouldn't—well, you wouldn't take him back, would you?' she asked. 'Oh, darling, don't let him hurt you again.'

'I don't intend to.' Catherine could speak quite confidently now. 'Neil and I are finished. Totally.'

'Well!' Her mother's eyes gleamed appreciatively. 'I'm pleased to hear it. Little weasel! I never did like him.'

Which was true, thought Catherine ruefully. Mrs Lambert had always had her doubts about Neil's character, and, when he had left Catherine for his secretary, she had been the first to denounce him. Not that she hadn't harboured a sneaking relief when the divorce went through, Catherine acknowledged now. But she had supported her daughter all through that terrible time.

'Anyway, I suppose I ought to be going,' Mrs Lambert said, finishing her tea and refusing a second cup. 'I don't want Billy to have to stand around waiting for me. The secret of a successful relationship is to know when to make the right moves, and keeping him hanging about in the cold is not a good idea.'

Catherine had to smile, her mother's incorrigibility breaking through her own black mood, and bringing a trace of humour to her face. If only she were more like her mother, she reflected. Her mother wouldn't be sitting here, wondering what Morgan was doing, and whether she was ever going to see him again. She'd have balanced her needs against his, and if the scales had come down on her side, she'd have done something about it...

An hour later, Catherine left the house to get into the cab that was waiting at the gate. 'Jermyn Gate,' she said, hoping the driver would not ask her where it was, and, slamming the door behind her, she sank back against the leather upholstery.

Already, the doubts were nagging at her, and half a dozen times during the journey from her house to the West End she had to steel herself not to ask the driver to turn the cab around, and take her home again. But, somehow, she restrained herself from doing so, and as the lights of the city closed around them she accepted the fact that she was committed.

She looked down at herself instead, wondering if she should have worn something a little more formal. The close-fitting black trousers were flattering, and that was why she had chosen them. They accentuated the graceful length of her legs. But whether she should have teamed them with a wrap-around white sweater was something else. She hoped he wouldn't think the generous cleavage it exposed was a deliberate come-on. She zipped her soft leather jacket just a little higher, and hoped she didn't look too much like the black widow.

'Is this it?'

The cab driver had turned into a lamplit square, and stopped beside a fairly new block of luxury apartments. Catherine looked up at the towering skyscraper, with the words 'Jermyn Gate' written in gold letters on a white-painted sign in the forecourt, and nodded her head.

Thrusting open the door, she climbed out and paid the fare. She was tempted to ask him to wait, but that seemed an unnecessary safeguard. After all, if Morgan wasn't in—or didn't want to speak to her, she appended tensely—she could always pick up another cab. In this part of London, they were often running around, and, if not, she could always call a minicab.

However, her first obstacle proved not to be Morgan himself, but the commissionaire who apparently vetted all callers. 'Is Mr Lynch expecting you, miss?' he enquired, his manner not exactly insulting, but not exactly courteous either. Did Morgan often have young women coming asking to see him? she wondered uneasily. And if so, what on earth was she doing here?

'Er—no,' she admitted now, half prepared to beat a hasty retreat, but the commissionaire was already picking up the phone.

'I'll just tell him you're here, miss,' he said. 'What was the name?' And Catherine, who didn't want to give it, told him, simply because not to do so might have convinced him she was some kind of unsavoury character.

The phone rang for some time before it was answered, and Catherine was just beginning to believe she had been granted a reprieve, when the connection was made. 'There's a Miss Catherine Lambert here to see you, sir,' she heard the commissionaire say, in an insufferably deferential tone. 'She says you're not expecting her. Do you want me to send her up?'

Catherine couldn't hear Morgan's reply, and she was trying to decide whether it would be better if he refused to see her, or if he let her in, when the commissionaire replaced his receiver.

'You can go up, Miss Lambert,' he said, with considerably more warmth to his voice. 'The eighteenth floor. Number five.'

'Yes, I do know that,' said Catherine tersely, walking rather jerkily across to the lifts. Well, she really had burned her bridges behind her now, she thought. Dear God, please let her not make a fool of herself!

The corridor was carpeted in a deep green pile, a luxury she had never experienced in any other apartment

building she had visited. And Morgan's door had the
number on it in little gold figures. Nothing ostentatious,
of course. Just plain cardinal numbers. Daunting, all
the same, she thought, lifting her hand to tap at the
panels, and then stepped back aghast, when the door
was opened.

Morgan was wearing a bathrobe, and she guessed that
was why he had taken so long to answer the phone. His
hair was damp and tousled, his legs and feet, below the
hem of the robe, bare. But he was just as disturbing to
her emotional balance as ever, and, pushing her hands
into the pockets of her jacket, she endeavoured to adopt
a casual pose.

'Hello.'

'Hi.' The tawny eyes moved over her face with disruptive intensity, and settled on her mouth. 'Come in.'

'May I?'

Catherine's mouth was dry, but Morgan's invitation
was sincere. 'How could I refuse?' he countered, stepping
back to allow her to enter the hallway. 'You didn't.'

'What?' Catherine blinked behind the lenses of her
spectacles. 'Oh—no.' Understanding his meaning, she
acknowledged the irony. 'Thank you.'

The hall was wide and spacious, nothing like her hall,
with its narrow passageway along to the kitchen. What
was more, a curving staircase indicated a second floor
above, with a crystal chandelier suspended above it that
glinted with a thousand prisms of light.

She had no time to absorb any more than this before
Morgan closed the door behind them, and came to lead
the way into an equally impressive drawing-room. At
least, Catherine would have called it a drawing-room.
She wasn't sure what Morgan would call it. She only
knew there was a silky Persian carpet on the floor, and
a rich mixture of fine wood and leather in the chairs and
cabinets that furnished it. There was a sofa, too, up

holstered in a deep burgundy velvet, and curtains of a matching shade hanging at the long windows.

'Like it?' Morgan asked, and Catherine, who had been thinking how the apartment mirrored the enormous gulf between them, gave a nervous nod of her head.

'It's beautiful,' she said politely. 'I—had no idea it would be like this.'

'Didn't you?' Morgan's expression was unreadable. 'Well...' He indicated the tray of drinks residing on the top of a polished cabinet. 'Do you want a drink? I could use one.'

'Why? Because I'm here?'

The words just slipped out, and Catherine's nails dug into her palms as Morgan's eyes narrowed in sudden contempt. 'Could be,' he responded coolly. 'You should have phoned before you left home.'

Catherine held up her head. 'So you could have stopped me from coming?'

'Perhaps.'

Morgan was non-committal, and it was only the thought of confronting that supercilious commission-aire again that kept her where she was. This had not been a good idea, she thought, trying not to blame her mother for unknowingly putting the thought into her head.

He shrugged now. 'So, what'll it be? Scotch? Gin?'

Catherine wanted to refuse, but she thought having a drink in her hand might make her feel a little less tense. 'Do—er—do you have any sherry?' she asked, and when he gave her an old-fashioned look she said quickly, 'Oh—Scotch, then. No ice.'

He poured her drink and gave it to her, their fingers touching as the glass changed hands. The contact caused a shiver of awareness to run up her arm, and she wrapped both hands around the glass.

Morgan poured Scotch for himself, a generous measure which he threw to the back of his throat.

Catherine was sure he couldn't have tasted it, but that didn't stop him pouring himself another before turning to face her again.

'Sit down,' he said, gesturing with his glass. 'As you're here, the least we can be is civil.'

Catherine hesitated, and then cautiously seated herself on the edge of a buttoned armchair. Now that she was here, she didn't know how to handle it, and it crossed her mind, belatedly, that he might not have been alone. She should have phoned, she thought unhappily. After all, as far as she knew, Morgan hadn't intended to see her again. She had allowed a totally unsolicited sense of responsibility for him to get the better of her common sense.

'Now,' he said, propping his hips against a mahogany bureau, 'Do you want to tell me what you're doing here?'

Catherine looked up at him uneasily. She had expected that he would sit down, too, but, although he hadn't, she didn't feel capable of getting up again. Instead, she found her eyes moving over him almost hungrily, noticing how his navy-blue bathrobe accentuated his dark masculinity. She knew it was ridiculous, but she hadn't realised until now how much she had needed to see him, and the urge to tell him was only barely controllable.

Something of what she was feeling must have showed in her eyes, however, for with an oath Morgan moved away from her. 'Don't,' he said roughly, and she didn't need any more elaboration to know what he meant. 'You're wasting your time.'

Catherine got up then, feeling as if she were some particularly obnoxious kind of insect, and he had just put his foot on her. The heat in her stomach gave way to an unnatural sense of chill, and, even though she swallowed the remaining Scotch in her glass, in an effort to stop the blood from congealing in her veins, she doubted she would ever feel warm again.

'I'm sorry,' she said, putting down her glass and making for the door. 'I shouldn't have come here.'

'Why did you?'

His question deserved an answer, and although Catherine didn't feel much like giving one she paused in the doorway and looked back at him. 'I wanted to see you,' she said flatly. She touched her spectacles. 'Stupid, wasn't it?'

Morgan regarded her through narrowed eyes. 'Why?' he enquired harshly. 'Because you feel safe with me now?'

Catherine blinked. 'I beg your pardon?'

'Oh, don't pretend you haven't been asking Kay questions about me! I wouldn't answer you, so you got Kay to tell you. I guess you two had a real good bitch about poor old Morgan!'

'That's not true!' Catherine turned back into the room. 'I didn't ask Kay anything. *She*—she insisted on telling me.'

'Really?'

'Yes, really.' Catherine tucked her hair behind her ear with a nervous hand. 'What do you think I am?'

'I guess it's more a question of what you think I am,' retorted Morgan, pouring himself a third measure of Scotch. 'Damn it—I am what I am. It doesn't really matter how you found out.'

Catherine stared at him. 'Found out what? That you served in Vietnam? That you were captured by the Vietcong? So what? It's not something to be ashamed of.'

Morgan's lips took on a cynical twist. 'The ubiquitous do-gooder!' he taunted scathingly. Do you know how sick I am of understanding women?'

Catherine flinched, but she refused to let him have the last word. 'Better a do-gooder than someone who pities himself,' she retorted, standing her ground, even when he left the tray of drinks and came towards her. 'You

can't offend me, Mr Lynch.' She took a steadying breath.
'You—might make me feel sorry for you——'

'I don't need anyone to feel sorry for me,' he snarled,
halting in front of her, and, although she had spoken
confidently enough, Catherine was practically shaking
in her boots.

'Then stop—stop behaving as if you were the only
veteran with—with——'

'With what?' He thrust his face close to hers, and she
could smell the scent of whisky on his breath.

'With—problems,' she finished, in a small voice, and
Morgan closed his eyes.

At once, Catherine wanted to cut out her tongue. She
hated saying these things to him; she hated hurting him.
Dear God, she had thought she would have done anything to try and make things easier for him, and she
hated the thought that he might think she was simply
curious.

'Morgan . . .'

Acting purely on impulse, she put her fingers up to
his face, cupping it between her hands, and bringing her
mouth to his. His eyes opened then, the dark pupils
dilating as they bored into hers. He didn't move,
however. He merely stood there, letting Catherine run
her nervous tongue over his lips.

And then, when her failing confidence reminded her
that she was no good at this sort of thing, and she would
have drawn back, his hands slid inside the neck of her
jacket, and closed about her throat.

She wasn't scared. Amazingly, considering her
awareness of his strength, the knowledge that he could
snap her neck as easily as he might break a twig didn't
frighten her. On the contrary, the feel of those hard
hands around her throat was wonderfully familiar. And
she swayed against him.

'Cat,' he said, and now his tone was thick with
emotion, 'this is not a good idea.'

'Isn't it?' Unzipping her jacket, she dropped it off her shoulders, and slipped her arms around his neck. 'Kiss me, Morgan. *Please*!'

She would never have believed she could act so shamelessly, but she was beyond the point of worrying about her reputation. She had rejected any modesty by coming here, and, if begging him to touch her was unsophisticated, then so be it.

'You—don't—understand,' he said in a strangled voice, but when he looked down at the dusky hollow between her breasts she saw only raw need in his eyes. He wanted her; she knew it, and almost as an afterthought she realised she wanted him. Until then, it had been his pain, his anguish, she had been trying to assuage. Oh, she had wanted him to kiss her, to touch her, but anything else had been purely incidental. Making love with Neil had taught her that foreplay was everything, and what came after had mostly been an anticlimax. Indeed, she had come to the conclusion that a woman's expectations, and their lack of realisation, formed the origin of that word. The occasions when she had felt some satisfaction had been few and far between. But this was nothing like anything she had felt before. Now, she was experiencing a totally different feeling. Every nerve in her body was alive and tingling with the awareness of Morgan's lean muscled frame, and a moist ache invaded her lower limbs.

'Don't talk ****' he said savagely, using an expletive she had never realised could have such a sexual connotation, his hands on her hips burning through the fine material of her trousers. His hands were sure and sensuous, the soft jersey only a small barrier to his hard fingers.

With undisguised urgency he covered her lips with his, and Catherine's mouth opened beneath his demanding tongue. She wanted his tongue in her mouth, she thought mindlessly. She wanted to feel him, and taste him, and her own tongue joined his in a sensual imitation of possession.

Her hands gripped the damp hair at his nape, and then slipped inside his bathrobe to caress the warm-scented skin of his shoulders. She hadn't known a man's skin could be so smooth and silky, and when he released her mouth she turned her lips against his neck. She wanted to kiss him all over, she thought fancifully, as his harsh breathing moistened her ear. He was so beautiful, so beautifully male, and the hot core inside her throbbed in anticipation.

Her hands trembling a little, she allowed her fingers to slide down the lapels of his bathrobe, parting the material as they went, and exposing his chest to her lips. His chest was broad and muscled, and only slightly spread with curling dark hair. Like his arms and legs, it was deeply tanned, but the tips of hair were bleached a lighter shade.

However, when her exploration reached the knotted belt at his waist, his fingers came to grip hers with grim determination. 'No,' he said, in a hoarse, unnatural tone, and she looked up to find his face was pale and streaked with sweat.

'Morgan?' she questioned uncomprehendingly, still not willing to believe he meant to stop her, but, with a constricted sound, he put her away from him. Half turning away from her, he wrapped the folds of the bathrobe more closely about him, and Catherine was left feeling like an unsuccessful courtesan.

'I'm sorry,' he said, his voice sounding as if it had been dredged up from some place deep inside him. 'That—shouldn't have happened.'

CHAPTER NINE

IF SHE hadn't felt so utterly humiliated, Catherine could have laughed. Wasn't it usually the woman who said that? Instead of which, she was the one who had been made to feel as if she had taken unwelcome liberties.

Finding her spectacles on the chair, she pushed them on to her nose. Not that it wouldn't have been easier to leave them off, she thought. Without her spectacles, everything beyond a certain distance developed a slight haze around it, and just now she would have preferred that imprecise aspect. The last thing she wanted to see was Morgan's contempt, and, keeping her eyes averted, she bent and picked up her jacket.

She hadn't brought a handbag. Just her purse, which was safely zipped inside her pocket, and, trailing the jacket behind her, she walked out of the room. If she could just make it out of the building, she told herself encouragingly. She refused to let that supercilious commissionaire see that she was crying.

She didn't even make it to the lift. She was reaching for the Yale lock on the outer door when Morgan's hand reached past her head, to prevent her from opening it. 'Don't go,' he said, his lips against her hair, and she swung round and slumped back against the panels, her eyes raw with unshed tears. 'Don't go,' he said again and when she gazed up at him in total confusion he bent his head and gave her a lingering kiss.

She tried not to respond to him. She had already had one disappointment, and she didn't think she could take another. It was too bewildering, too shattering, too much of everything she had sworn to avoid. Getting involved could be painful; with Morgan, it was downright dangerous. He made her do things she had never done before; made her feel things she had never felt before; and he made her want something she was very much afraid she could never have.

But Morgan's lips were too demanding—too persuasive—to resist, and, once again, she felt her defences tumbling. He had only to touch her, and the blood ran like liquid fire through her veins. With a little moan of protest, she wound her arms around his neck and kissed him back, and Morgan bent and put one arm behind her knees and swung her off her feet.

Keeping his mouth on hers, he carried her up the stairs, but Catherine was too bemused to notice where he was taking her. Her only contribution was to remove her spectacles again, and they dropped from her hand, to land unnoticed on the bottom stair.

She opened her eyes when she felt the soft texture of silk at her back. The short, wrap-around sweater had bared her midriff, and she felt the cool sheets against her spine. Morgan had laid her on an enormous bed— his bed, she surmised, with a *frisson* of excitement—and he came down on it beside her, stifling any comment she might have made beneath the urgent pressure of his lips.

She wanted to protest that she was still wearing her boots, and that their soles might soil the satin quilt that her outstretched hands had encountered, but such mundane considerations were soon outweighed by other, more important matters. Morgan's mouth had moved from hers to slide down the slender column of her throat, and her skin burned where his lips touched.

She was sure she must look a blotchy mess, but Morgan only murmured, 'Beautiful,' as he cupped her breasts in his hands, and brought one burgeoning nipple to his mouth. The hard little peak surged against the taut cloth, and it was an immense relief when he slipped his hand inside her sweater and her bra, and freed the swollen flesh.

'How does this thing come off?' he mumbled, her nipple in his mouth, and Catherine fumbled behind her to release the woollen ties.

Once she was without her sweater, and the lacy scrap of bra, Morgan took full advantage of her responsive breasts, caressing them sensuously, and suckling at each of them in turn. To Catherine, who had never experienced this kind of excitement before, every tug of his tongue or teeth caused a sharp pain in the pit of her stomach. It was not an unpleasant pain; in fact, it was excessively enjoyable, and she moved against him urgently, arching her back to bring her into closer contact with his lean body. But Morgan resisted her efforts to wind her legs about him. Pressing her back again, his hands found the zipper of her tight trousers and, opening it, he began to peel them down over her hips.

Her boots were discarded without her needing to say anything, dropping on to the floor at the foot of the bed with a distinctive thud. Then her trousers followed them, and Morgan's teeth skimmed the elasticated waist of her panties.

Catherine felt as if she was burning up. Every inch of her body was sensitised to the sensual brush of his lips, all her nerves straining to meet his every demand. With infinite patience, Morgan used his teeth to tug her panties away, his lips seeking the dusky curls at the junction of her legs, while his fingers completed the process. Then, when her nervous fingers dug protestingly into his shoulders, he slid back over her, his mouth finding hers once again.

'Good?' he murmured, and Catherine nodded vigorously.

'Good,' she echoed, finding it difficult to say anything, with his hand between her legs bringing her to the brink of a frenzied spasm. 'Mor-gan,' she choked, trying to tell him she wanted to share this with him, but it was too late. She was beyond reason, beyond restraint, spinning out of control over the precipice of her emotions...

She came down to earth all too soon, to find Morgan lying on his back beside her. Like hers, his skin was damp and cool, but she didn't need a lot of experience to know that he had not shared her delight. The pleasure he had given her had been entirely one-sided, and she blinked her eyes bewilderedly, as she struggled up on to one elbow. Why had he done what he did? she wondered, looking down into his face with troubled eyes. His eyes were closed, but she could tell he was not asleep. He was breathing too quickly for that, his chest rising and falling beneath the loosely drawn folds of his bathrobe. She could have sworn he *had* wanted her. Had she done something wrong?

'Morgan,' she breathed now, bending her head and touching her lips to the warm hollow of his neck. 'Morgan—what's wrong?'

He opened his eyes then, and, although she had been afraid that he might be angry with her, his expression was warmly indulgent. 'Nothing's wrong,' he said, though there was some tension in his tone. 'Are you all right?'

Catherine caught her lower lip between her teeth. 'Why did you do it?' she exclaimed, instead of answering him. 'Why didn't you...?' She pressed her lips together. 'I wanted you inside me, when——'

Morgan's expression darkened. 'Didn't I please you?'

'Of course you pleased me.' Catherine smoothed back the damp hair from his forehead. 'But you could have pleased me a lot more——'

'No, I couldn't.' Morgan rolled away from her, and sat up, drawing one leg towards his chest, and resting his chin on his knee. 'That's what I've been trying to

tell you. I don't—that is——' He broke off for a
moment, and then continued harshly, 'I'm useless to a
woman!'

Catherine stared at him. 'I—don't believe that.'

'It's true.' Morgan gave her a cool, indifferent stare.
'It's not something I'd lie about, believe me!'

Catherine moved her head from side to side. 'But—
there must be something you can do——?'

'No.' Morgan was adamant. 'I'm sorry you had to
find out this way, but there it is.' He paused. 'But I'd
be grateful if you didn't broadcast the news. I don't have
much, but I do have a little pride.'

'Oh, Morgan!'

Catherine scrambled on to her knees, and would have
put her arms around him and hugged him, but he held
her off. 'Don't,' he said quellingly, and now there was
no warmth in his gaze. 'I don't want your sympathy. I
don't need it. I'm lucky, really. I still have my health,
and strength, and all my faculties, such as they are. Believe me, not everyone's so lucky.'

Catherine shivered. 'Oh, Morgan!'

'Don't look at me like that!' With a muffled oath, he
swung off the bed, crossing the room to stand with his
back to her, at the windows. 'I think you'd better go,'
he said heavily. 'I'll call you a cab.'

Catherine hesitated. 'Can't we talk about this?'

'What's there to say?' He didn't turn.

'Well...' Catherine stared helplessly around her. 'Is
there nothing I can do to help you?'

'There's nothing anyone can do to help me,' replied
Morgan flatly. 'Do you think they haven't tried?'

'No, but...' Catherine slid to the edge of the bed now,
realising how unselfconscious she was of her nakedness
with him. 'I could try to help.'

'How?' He spun around then, staring at her with impatient eyes, and Catherine's brief spell of positive
thinking evaporated. With fumbling hands she searched

for her bra and panties, half turning away from him as she did so, to avoid his contemptuous gaze.

'Here,' he said, his voice sounding immeasurably closer, and she glanced behind her to find him squatting beside the bed. He was holding her flimsy scraps of underwear out to her, and, taking them from him, she endeavoured to put them on. But her hands betrayed her once again, and, although she managed to step into her panties, Morgan was obliged to fasten her bra for her.

'What a novelty,' he said drily, handing her her sweater. 'A man usually takes a woman's clothes off. He doesn't help her to put them on again. But then, I'm not a man, am I?' he added, getting to his feet, and returning to his stance at the windows.

'Well, I'm not a woman!' blurted Catherine tremulously, and again he turned to give her a scathing glance. 'What are you talking about?'

'I mean it,' said Catherine fiercely, zipping up her trousers. She reached for her boots, as much to avoid looking at him as anything. 'I—I can't have children. I'm—barren. Isn't that what they call it, in the Bible? I can't fulfil my function in life.'

'Oh, God!' Morgan's expression softened, and he shook his head. 'You didn't have to tell me that!'

Catherine bent her head, pulling on her boots. 'I wanted to,' she said simply. 'Apart—apart from Neil—and my mother—I've never told anyone else.'

Morgan groaned, but he didn't move. 'I'm sorry.'

'Are you?' Catherine looked at him then. 'Well, like you, I don't like sympathy either. It's just one of those things. A freak of nature, I suppose.'

'It's not *that* important,' said Morgan quietly.

'Isn't it?' Catherine got to her feet. 'It's why Neil walked out on me. He wanted children, you see, and I couldn't give him them.'

Morgan's lips curled. 'Then he's crazy!'

'What do you mean?'

'Leaving you, because you couldn't have a baby.' Morgan made an anguished sound. 'It wouldn't matter to me. If I could have you, I'd consider myself a happy man.'

Catherine caught her breath. 'If you...but—you can have me,' she exclaimed, covering the space between them, but Morgan backed away.

'No. No, I can't,' he said intractably.

'Why not?' Catherine was pleading with him, but she didn't care. She loved him. Oh, God, *she loved him*! she realised shatteringly. Whatever he was, whatever he had done, whatever had been done to him, she loved him, desperately. And he was sending her away. She knew he was.

'It wouldn't work.' His tone was dogged. 'I wouldn't do that to you.'

'What you are doing to me is worse,' protested Catherine helplessly. 'Oh, Morgan, don't—don't say we can't see one another again. You—you started this. It isn't fair!'

'I tried to finish it,' Morgan reminded her wearily. 'I didn't ask you to come here. You came of your own volition.'

Catherine spread her hands. 'But—you didn't send me away!'

'God!' Morgan cast his eyes towards the ceiling. 'What do you expect of me, Cat? I may be only half a man, but I am human! I wanted to send you away, but I couldn't do it. I care about you, for God's sake! Hurting you is like hurting myself!'

Catherine's lips parted. 'Then...'

'Go home, Cat,' he intoned tiredly. 'We had—what we had, but now it's over. Find yourself a man who can love you—in every way. You deserve it. Between us, Neil and me, we've really screwed up your life!'

* * *

She broke her spectacles in her flight down the stairs. There was only so much she could take without breaking herself, and the flimsy frames crumpled beneath her boot. She picked them up, of course, and, when she did so, she saw Morgan watching her from the top of the stairs. But he said nothing, and nor did she. There was nothing more to say.

Of course, in the cab going back to Orchard Road Catherine told herself he didn't mean it. He couldn't. Sooner or later, his will would crack, and then he'd come and find her. He cared about her. He had said so. That had to mean something. He couldn't throw it all away.

But, in the weeks that followed, that belief was slowly eroded. In spite of her conviction that he would come after her, he didn't. Once again, she was reduced to losing her breath every time the phone rang, or her heart skipping a beat when someone came to the door. But, as before, disappointment always followed anticipation, and slowly but surely she was compelled to acknowledge the superior strength of his will. He had meant what he said. Their brief affair was over.

That was when she started to develop other symptoms. Although during daylight hours she managed to withstand the agony of emotional withdrawal, the hours of darkness posed an entirely different problem. She grew to resent having to go home to her little house in the evening. She began staying at her desk, long after her colleagues had gone home, working sometimes until the building supervisor came to lock up.

Of course, she accomplished a lot of work; not all of it good, but most of it adequate. And, because she was always willing, people began to take advantage of her. It wasn't that they were particularly selfish, she realised. It was just that they had lives to lead outside the office, and if she was prepared to shoulder some of their responsibilities, it gave them more time to spend with their families—or lovers.

Naturally, she didn't actually put this into words. It would have been too painful to consider what it really meant. She didn't want to think of other people sharing their lives. Her own life was so sterile that she even found watching couples together on television almost more than she could bear. No; she steeled her mind to concentrate only on the evaluations she made, declining all offers to socialise with an indifference that bordered on psychopathic.

Nevertheless, eventually, she was always compelled to go home, and, when she did, Hector greeted her like a long-lost friend. She knew that in his feline way he must know something was wrong. Cats were very intelligent, and she had never neglected him in the past. Indeed, he had always been her ally, her friend, her bastion against loneliness. His company had compensated her for Neil's absence, but he could never compensate her for Morgan's. And, in the dark reaches of the night, the memories of what she and Morgan had had—*and what they might have had*—tore her emotions to shreds.

She supposed it would have been better if she had never tasted what she was missing. Until Morgan had taken her to bed, that side of a relationship was not something she had thought she needed. When she had missed Neil, it had been his company she had coveted, the companionship of knowing someone else was in the house. Hector had filled that space fairly satisfactorily, and if she had missed having someone to talk to she had got over it.

But Morgan was something else. In a few days he had achieved what Neil had been unable to achieve in almost five years of marriage, and she was absolutely desolate. She ached for him; she literally ached with the needs he had aroused in her. She would have given anything just to be able to see him, to touch him, to feel his arms around her. Some nights, her skin felt so hot and vulnerable that it was as if she had exposed an open wound.

How could he do this to her? she wondered. How could he do it to himself?

Apart from the men at work, who probably thought her change of temperament signalled some kind of premature menopause, her Aunt Agnes was the first to notice that something was seriously wrong. Her mother was always so busy with her life, and, although she suspected Catherine wasn't happy, she assumed Neil was at the back of it. She was more concerned about the fact that her daughter was losing weight, and every time they met she asked if Catherine had seen a doctor yet.

But her father's sister, who called unexpectedly one Saturday afternoon, and found her niece sitting in the front room, staring blindly at the television, was infinitely more astute. The unnatural tidiness of the house, the hollows beneath Catherine's eyes, and the lack of any kind of expression in her voice, disturbed her deeply. Her niece had always been such a level-headed young woman, and, although she had been upset when her husband had walked out on her, she had never lost her sense of humour. Now, however, she was like an automaton, and, although Agnes Lambert was a pragmatist, she guessed instinctively that the problem was an emotional one.

'Who is he?' she asked pleasantly, after having prepared them both a cup of tea, and carried it into the sitting-room. 'You might feel better if you talk about it.'

Although her words were not dissimilar to her mother's, Catherine didn't do her the injustice of pretending not to understand. 'I can't,' she said flatly. 'I want to. But I can't.'

Agnes frowned. 'I see.' She surveyed her niece critically. In close-fitting woolly tights, and a thigh-length cardigan, Catherine's narrowing hips were sharply defined. 'I suppose that's why you're losing weight. Are you eating?'

Catherine flushed. 'Enough,' she said, picking up her teacup and forcing herself to drink the hot sweet beverage her aunt had prepared. 'I'm not hungry most of the time.' She grimaced. 'Good diet, eh? I should write a book.'

'Hmm.' Her aunt was thoughtful. 'How long has this been going on?'

'What?' Now Catherine did prevaricate, but her aunt's expression caused her to utter a rueful sigh. 'I don't know,' she said wearily. 'Five or six weeks, I suppose. I—I knew someone. Back in October. But it only lasted a very short time.'

'And in three weeks it will be Christmas,' remarked Agnes dauntingly. 'Catherine, this can't go on. Does your mother know what's happening? I can't believe she hasn't noticed.'

Catherine shook her head. 'She's noticed I've lost weight.'

'And?'

'She thinks it's still Neil.'

'But it's not.'

'No.'

'But it is a man?'

'Yes.' Catherine put down her cup and buried her face in her hands.

'Oh, my dear...' Agnes put down her own cup, and left her seat to comfort her niece. 'My dear, you've got to talk to someone. If you don't—well, I don't think you can take much more.'

'I can't.' Catherine pressed the heels of her hands against her eyes, but the hot tears squeezed out anyway.

'You can't what?' Her aunt's arm about her shoulders was very supportive.

'I can't—take—much—more,' said Catherine, her throat constricting. 'What am I going to do, Aunt Agnes? I love him, and—it's *hopeless*!'

Her aunt hugged her closer. 'He's married?'

'No.'

'But—there is someone else?'

Catherine shook her head. 'I don't think so.'

'I see.' Agnes looked puzzled. 'So—doesn't he love you?'

Catherine lifted her head, her face pale and streaked with tears. 'Yes,' she said wildly. 'Yes, he does. At least, he said he cared about me. But you don't understand...' She licked a tear from her lips. 'He—he's been ill.'

'Ill?' Her aunt was getting more and more confused, and, realising she had to explain at least a little of what she was talking about, Catherine nodded.

'He's an American,' she said carefully. 'He—works here, in London.'

'At the Embassy?'

'Why, yes.' Catherine frowned. 'How did you know?'

'I didn't,' admitted her aunt ruefully. 'It was just a guess. Go on.'

Catherine hesitated. 'Well—as I said, he's been ill.'

'How ill?' Her aunt was wary.

'Psychologically, I think,' said Catherine, trying to be honest. If her aunt was going to be shocked, then so be it. 'He was in Vietnam. And—part of the time, he was in a Vietcong prison camp.'

Agnes drew back to her seat. 'Oh, Catherine!' she said weakly. 'My dear, I don't know what to say.'

Catherine wiped the tears off her cheeks, and looked at the older woman with empty eyes. 'I suppose you think I'm well out of it, don't you?'

Agnes shook her head. 'Having never met this man, I wouldn't like to make such a generalisation,' she replied. 'And—this is why he...well, why you're not seeing one another any more?'

Catherine bent her head. 'Partly.' She sniffed. 'Oh, Aunt Agnes, I wish you could meet him. You'd like him, I know you would. I've never known anyone like him before. He made me realise that I never loved Neil—not in the way you're supposed to love someone anyway. Oh—I know this probably sounds very unlikely to you, but——'

'I'm not completely without imagination,' protested her aunt drily. And then, more seriously, 'I knew someone once. As a matter of fact, we were going to get married. But...' she shrugged. '...he was killed in Korea. It was never the same with anyone else.'

'Really?' Catherine stared at her aunt now, realising that in all the years she had known her she had always taken her mother's opinion of Agnes's desire to remain single as gospel. It had never occurred to her that her father's tall, thin, capable sister might once have been as vulnerable as she was herself. 'I'm sorry.'

'Don't be.' Agnes was practical. 'It all happened a long time ago. It probably wouldn't have worked out. But, there we are: it happened, and I survived. Just.'

Catherine managed a watery smile. 'Thank you.'

'Has it helped at all?'

'Some.' At least Catherine didn't feel quite so knotted up inside. 'Will you stay to tea?'

'If you promise to eat something, too,' Agnes agreed. 'And now, let's go for a walk, shall we? It's a cold day, but it's dry. And I think you could do with some fresh air.'

CHAPTER TEN

A WEEK later, Catherine drove to Morgan's apartment.

It hadn't been her destination when she left the house—or she didn't think it had; not consciously, anyway—but it was Sunday afternoon, the roads were comparatively quiet, and she found herself turning naturally towards Jermyn Gate.

Not that she intended to run the risk of entering the building again. Apart from the fact that she was sure Morgan would refuse to see her—and the fragile shell which Aunt Agnes was helping her build around herself wouldn't take that kind of rejection—she wanted to dispel the memory of how she had left here on that terrible evening, when Morgan had delivered his ultimatum. She had run out of the building, clutching her broken spectacles, and she was sure the commissionaire had thought Morgan had assaulted her.

There were few cars parked in Jermyn Gate this Sunday afternoon. Like other modern apartment buildings in London, the cars owned by the residents were housed in the underground garage, and only the visitors' cars occupied the limited parking spaces on the forecourt.

Catherine halted a few yards from the forecourt of the building. Although it was unlikely, she didn't want Morgan looking out of his window and recognising the car. Not that it was likely, she reflected impatiently. There must be at least a hundred navy-blue Peugeots in this area of the city alone, and the night Morgan had ridden in her car he had been in no state to notice its colour or its designation.

Turning off the engine, she drew a steadying breath. Well, she was here, she thought tautly. There was the building, and if she looked up eighteen floors she could probably identify his apartment. Not that she had actually looked out of the window, she reflected. But the very size of it dictated that, by the law of averages, she was almost certain to be able to see his windows.

But she didn't look. Like a patient with a phobia, she decided that actually coming here was enough to be going on with. It would be something positive she could tell Aunt Agnes. She had actually parked within a stone's throw of Morgan's apartment building without falling apart.

And then she saw him. He came out of the building, and walked across to where the cars were parked. His shoulders were hunched inside a camel-hair overcoat, and he was wearing a hat, but it was him. She was sure of it. And when he stopped beside a sleek Mercedes and started searching his pockets for his keys, she thrust open her door and got out.

This was not something Aunt Agnes would have approved of, she thought, as she ran towards him. But it seemed like fate that he should have emerged at just that moment, and she would not have been human if she hadn't felt that irresistible urge to speak to him. Just this one time...

He found his keys, and walked round the car. Any minute, he was going to get inside, and her opportunity would be lost. Not hesitating, not thinking, acting purely on impulse, she called his name, and when he turned to look at her, the bottom fell out of her world.

It wasn't Morgan. Oh, it was like him. The height and build were very similar, but this man was older, much older. And there was no trace of recognition in the enquiring eyes that turned in her direction.

'I'm—sorry...' Catherine halted uncertainly, her chest heaving, her spectacles sliding down the perspiration that had beaded on her nose. 'I—thought you were someone else.'

She turned away, pain and exhaustion making a mockery of her bid for rehabilitation. She felt almost as bad now as she had done that night she ran out of the building, and she shook her head despairingly when the man's voice arrested her. She didn't want to talk to him. She didn't want to talk to anybody.

'Miss,' he said, his accent unmistakably transatlantic in origin. 'Wait!' And when she reluctantly turned to face him he added, 'Are you looking for my son?'

Catherine's jaw sagged. 'Your—son?' she whispered disbelievingly.

'Yes, my son,' agreed the man, leaving the car and walking towards her. 'Morgan Lynch. Do you know where he is?'

Catherine felt faint. She was trembling so badly, she didn't know how her legs continued to support her. No wonder she had thought he looked like Morgan, she thought. The similarities were so obvious now that she looked for them.

'Do you know where he is?'

The man had reached her, and was looking down at her with cool, enquiring eyes. His attitude was polite enough, but she sensed his impatience when she continued to stare at him without speaking. She guessed he was not a man who took kindly to insubordination of any kind, and, remembering that Kay had told her that Morgan's father had been a US Army general, she realised how aggravating to him her attitude must be.

'I—no,' she said now, swaying a little, as the cold December afternoon chilled her sweating limbs. 'Isn't he here? I know this is where he lives.'

'Lived,' corrected Morgan's father, glancing over his shoulder. 'According to the doorman, my son hasn't been seen for over a month.'

'Oh, *God*!'

Catherine could feel a wave of blackness sweeping over her, and, realising she had to get back to her car before she collapsed, she put out a warning hand. But Morgan's father didn't respond in the way she expected. Instead of leaving her to make her own way to her car, he put his hand beneath her arm, and said, gently, 'Let me help you.'

Catherine was so dizzy that she scarcely cared where he was taking her. But when he opened the car door and helped her inside, she realised at once that this was not her Peugeot. Not that it was Morgan's car either, she realised now. It wasn't even the same colour. But it was similar, and when Morgan's father walked round and got in beside her, she had a peculiar sense of *déjà vu*.

'So,' he said, half turning in the seat beside her. 'Tell me where I can buy you a drink.'

'Oh—no. Really.' Catherine swallowed. 'There's no need for that.'

'I think there is,' retorted General Lynch, turning back to the wheel, and starting the engine. 'I'd suggest we use Morgan's apartment, if there was anything in it. But there isn't. He, and that Filipino who looks after him, haven't even left a bottle of Scotch to make it worthwhile.'

Catherine moistened her lips. 'You've—been in Morgan's apartment, then?'

'Yeah. That doorman opened up the place for me. He didn't want to. But when I told him I had friends at Scotland Yard he became a bit more co-operative.'

'I see.'

Catherine breathed a little more easily. While in one way it was devastating to think that, even if she was prepared to face his anger again, she wouldn't be able to find him, the alternative—that Morgan might be lying in his apartment, sick, or *worse*—didn't bear thinking about.

'I assume you're a friend of my son's, right?' the man beside her said now, and without any other option open to her, Catherine nodded. 'And you don't know where he is?'

'No.' The full weight of that realisation was beginning to bear down on her. 'No. I'm sorry.'

General Lynch cast her a thoughtful look. 'How long is it since you've seen him?'

'Oh—some time.' Catherine hoped she was not going to have to go into that. 'We—er—we agreed not to see one another for—for a while.' It was only half the truth. She couldn't tell him that Morgan had refused to see her again, could she?

Morgan's father nodded, and then, noticing a small restaurant in a side-street, he swung off the main thoroughfare. 'Will this do?'

Catherine shook her head. 'Honestly. If you could just take me back to Jermyn Gate——'

'I will,' he promised, stopping the car on double yellow lines, and pushing open his door. 'After we've had a drink.'

The waiter who met them at the door of the restaurant was most apologetic. Yes, he said, they had been open for the lunch period, but they were closing now. It was Sunday; they were sorry, but they had their licence to think about.

Two minutes later however, he was showing them to a candle-lit table in the window. Some notes—Catherine didn't know how many—had changed hands, and, with the utmost courtesy, they were invited to look at the menu.

'Just Scotch,' General Lynch declared, handing back the over-sized bills of fare. 'And brandy for the lady. That's all.'

'I don't want any brandy,' Catherine protested, but Morgan's father only quirked a greying eyebrow.

'I think you do,' he said drily. 'You nearly keeled over back there. Girls—*women*—of your age don't just pass out for no reason. I'm curious. What's wrong with you?'

He paused, and then added softly, 'You can't be pregnant?'

'No!' Catherine realised Morgan's father had the same directness of manner as his son, and it was no easier to deal with.

'OK.' There was a trace of regret in the old man's face, but he hid his feelings admirably. 'So—what is there between you two?' he persisted. 'Why should the news that Morgan's left the country make you want to faint?'

Catherine stared at him, her consternation evident. And then, after acknowledging the drink the waiter set in front of her, she exclaimed, 'How do you know he's left the country?'

'I don't. Not yet.' General Lynch studied the Scotch in his glass, before swallowing a mouthful. 'But I'd say it was a fair possibility. Wouldn't you?'

Catherine pressed a hand to her throat. 'I—don't know.' She hesitated a moment, and then ventured, 'Where would he go?'

'Mango Key?' suggested Morgan's father tentatively. 'What do you think?'

Catherine sat back in her chair. 'Mango Key?' She shook her head bewilderedly. 'Is that—is that in—Florida?'

'So he told you about that, did he?'

There was a wealth of hope in the old man's voice now, but Catherine had to disappoint him. 'No,' she said, stroking her thumb over the rim of her glass. 'Kay did. Kay Sawyer.'

'Ah.' General Lynch expelled his breath on a sigh. 'I thought it wasn't like Morgan to talk about himself.' He ran a weary hand over his jawline. 'For a minute I thought you and he had been . . . close.'

'We were!' Catherine couldn't let him think she was some kind of American groupie. 'We—oh—I thought something was—going to come of it.'

Morgan's father studied her doubtfully. 'Really?'

'Yes, really.' Catherine groaned, and then unable to prevent herself, she asked, 'Did you make him come to London?'

General Lynch looked a little formidable now. 'What business is that of yours?'

Catherine flushed, and then realising she had nothing to lose, she said unsteadily, 'Because I love him. And—and I don't think you understand him very well.'

'Don't you?' Morgan's father sounded ominous now. 'And why should you think that?'

Catherine bent her head. 'Because—oh, because I don't think he was ever happy here.'

'Not even with you?' There was definite sarcasm in his tone now, and Catherine's eyes sparkled with sudden anger.

'No. Not even with me,' she conceded painfully, and then found refuge in a little of the brandy.

'Then what were you doing at this apartment this afternoon?'

That was harder, and Catherine wet her lips before replying. 'We—we had an argument,' she said, wondering how she could tell him things she had never told anyone else, not even Aunt Agnes. 'Morgan said it wasn't . . . fair to me, to go on with our relationship. I—didn't agree.'

Morgan's father looked staggered. 'Then—you know . . .?'

Catherine didn't attempt to define what she knew. She just nodded, and the old man closed his eyes with sudden emotion. For a few moments he remained silent, marshalling his composure. And then, as she was about to tell him that a traffic warden was putting a parking ticket beneath the windscreen wiper of his car, he said, 'Morgan must have told you that. I don't think the Sawyers—well, I'm sure they didn't know.'

'No.' Catherine inclined her head. 'Yes, it was Morgan who told me. It was his way of ending our relationship.'

Her voice broke, and, as if understanding her distress, Morgan's father put his hand across the table, and squeezed her wrist reassuringly. 'You know...' He shook his head. 'Oh, I don't even know your name!'

'It's Catherine,' she said huskily. 'Catherine Lambert.'

'Well... Catherine? May I?' And at her nod of assent, he continued, 'It may be of some comfort to you to know that, as far as I know, my son has *never* divulged his ... condition ... to anyone.'

Catherine sniffed. 'I believe you, General.'

'General?' His blue eyes were wry. 'Now I'm sure Morgan didn't tell you that.'

'No.' Catherine forced a small smile. 'Your son doesn't talk much about himself, or his family.'

'Hmm.' He sighed. 'I suppose it was Kay who enlightened you. Is she a friend of yours?'

Catherine shrugged. 'We work for the same company. I've known her and Denzil for about five years, I suppose.'

'I see.' He nodded. 'You know then that Denzil is a sort of nephew of mine.'

'Yes.'

'Poor Denzil!' General Lynch's expression was resigned. 'I don't think he's ever forgiven Morgan for having a general for a father. Denzil's a career diplomat, and he would have so liked that distinction for himself.'

So that was why Denzil resented Morgan, Catherine thought. It explained a lot, not least his reasons for inviting Morgan to dinner. She didn't suppose Denzil ever forgot the influence General Lynch could exert.

'Anyway,' went on Morgan's father, 'it made his day when Morgan ran away and enlisted for Vietnam. I suppose he hoped he'd never come back.'

Catherine frowned. 'But why did Morgan run away and enlist?' she asked. And then, realising she was being abominably personal, she coloured. 'I'm sorry. Forget I asked. It's none of my business.'

'No. I'd like to tell you,' said the old man heavily. 'It's strange, but I have the feeling you know Morgan as well as anyone.' He propped his elbow on the table, and rested his chin on his knuckles. 'It was all my fault, you see. I drove him to it.'

Catherine blinked. 'You did?'

'Yes.' General Lynch considered his drink for a moment, and then he went on, 'Morgan's my only son, you see. My wife—God rest her soul!—and I had three daughters before Morgan was born.' He gave a short laugh. 'We'd almost given up hope of having a son, so you can imagine how delighted we were when Morgan came along.'

Catherine nodded, and he continued, 'His sisters were quite a bit older than he was. The eldest, Maggie, is nearly fifty; Rose and Elizabeth are a few years younger.' He paused. 'They spoiled him, of course. They'd always wanted a baby brother, and Morgan only had to lift a finger to have all three of them running to do his bidding.

'However, I didn't like it. I worried about him. About the influence four women would have on him as he got older.' He made a weary sound. 'I didn't want my son to grow up to be effeminate, lacking the kind of moral fibre I'd always instilled in the men of my command.'

He shook his head. 'Of course, I was wrong. Morgan was gentle, and sensitive, that's true, but never at any time did he exhibit any of the spineless tendencies I accused him of.'

Catherine caught her breath. 'You—accused him?'

'For my sins.' The old man shook his head. 'I wanted him to join the army, you see. I wanted him to go to West Point, as I had done. I wanted him to become an officer.' He lifted his shoulders. 'Morgan didn't want that. He had no time for the army. He wanted to go to UCLA—that's the University of Los Angeles—and study marine biology, for God's sake! I told him, he didn't have the brains to be a marine biologist!' He pulled a wry face. 'He said he supposed that was why I had become an army man.'

Catherine bit her lip. 'So—he ran away?'

'Not immediately, no.' This was obviously getting harder for his father to relate, and he swallowed the remainder of the Scotch in his glass before going on. 'There was a girl, you see.' He grimaced. 'There were always girls. I should have realised, a boy as . . . well, as sexually attractive as Morgan would have no trouble proving his masculinity, but I was—I still am—a stubborn old man.' He sighed. 'Anyway, this girl was totally unsuitable. A little gold-digger; it was obvious what she wanted. And she got it. When I forbade Morgan to see her again, it was the last straw.'

'But—he married her, didn't he?' ventured Catherine cautiously and Morgan's father conceded that he had.

'I should have known better than to forbid him to see her,' he said. 'I know that now. I knew it then, but it was too late. By the time I found out what was going on, they were married, and Morgan had enlisted.'

He made a harsh sound. 'Oh—I would have gotten him out again. I'd have moved heaven and earth to have him declared unfit to serve, but Morgan swore he'd never speak to me again if I used my influence to get him discharged. In consequence my wife invited Della—that was the girl's name—to move into our house in Arlington—that's near Washington—and Morgan went to Vietnam.' He brushed a hand across his face, as if the memory was too painful to bear. 'He was eighteen.'

'Eighteen!' Catherine remembered all those reports she had read about Vietnam. He had been so young.

'Yes, eighteen,' said General Lynch, determinedly strengthening his tone. 'He was twenty-five when he came back. And we hardly knew him.'

Catherine licked her lips. 'What about Della?'

'Oh . . .' Morgan's father made a dismissive gesture. 'She got a divorce, as soon as the news came through

that Morgan was missing, believed dead. My wife took
it the hardest. Not the divorce, you understand. We were
all glad to see the back of Della. But by then, Mary, my
wife, had discovered that she had cancer, and she knew
she would never see her son again. I think she lost the
will to live.'

Catherine felt so sorry for him. Not only had he lost
a son, or believed he had anyway, but he had lost his
wife, too. Some punishment! she thought.

'But—Morgan did come back,' she reminded him, and
he agreed.

'Yes. Morgan came back. But not the Morgan who
had gone away. It took some time for us—my daughters
and I—to realise that he wasn't going to get better
without professional help. They called it delayed stress
syndrome. But it wasn't just that. Morgan had spent
five years in a North Vietnamese prison camp. It was a
measure of his strength of will that he didn't lose his
mind.'

'But—he was ill.'

'Oh, yes. He suffered all the usual symptoms—alien-
ation, rage, guilt; but it was when he tried to commit
suicide that we realised he needed proper treatment. He
was hospitalised, and for six months we despaired of his
reason.

'But Morgan's a fighter.' He sniffed. 'Imagine me
saying that! Do you know, Catherine, my son has shown
more courage than I ever did. I fought in the last war,
I was with the liberation army that swept through France
and Belgium, but I never had the kind of experiences
Morgan had.'

He shook his head when the waiter came to ask if they
wanted another drink, and pushed his glass aside.
'Afterwards, when Morgan came home again, he asked
if he could go and work in Florida. A friend of his,
someone he knew before he went to Vietnam, had a

marina down there, and Morgan wanted to help him run it.'

'And you said no?' Catherine was horrified.

'No, I said yes,' said the general defensively. 'I let him stay there for—well, for more than five years. But, you have to understand, Catherine, Morgan is my son. I wanted him to be with me. And—when I thought he was fully recovered, I suggested he return to Washington.'

'And he did?'

'Oh, yes. You have to understand—since...well, since Vietnam, Morgan doesn't fight me any more. I don't say he doesn't want to fight me, but he kind of—humours me. Do you know what I mean? So—he came back to Washington, and, for a while, it was OK. But then—I could see the change in him, the restlessness. That was when I suggested to Denzil that he find him a job in London. I thought the change of scene might do what Washington couldn't. It seems I was wrong.'

Catherine shivered. 'What you said—Mango Key. That's where he was before, isn't it?'

'In Florida, yes. It's an island just off the gulf coast.' He grimaced. 'I've got an agent checking it out right now.'

'An agent?' Catherine frowned. 'Do you mean a private detective?'

'Something like that.' Morgan's father looked slightly shame-faced. 'I didn't want to run the risk of him seeing me and thinking I was keeping tabs on him.'

'But you are.'

'Only because I'm worried about him,' replied the general impatiently. 'Catherine, when Denzil eventually had the sense to tell me that Morgan hadn't been in to work for the past three weeks, I was desperate. I got the next flight to London, half afraid of what I'd find.'

'You thought he might have...?'

'I didn't know what to think. I only knew I had to come here and see for myself.'

'And the enquiry agent?'

'That was my way of covering all possibilities,' he said wearily. 'Do you have any idea what it's like spending hours in a plane, not knowing what you're going to find at the end of it?'

'No.' Catherine was honest. 'I've never crossed the Atlantic.'

The general regarded her with sudden intensity. 'Would you like to?'

Catherine gasped. 'What? To cross the Atlantic.' It seemed a totally inappropriate question.

'Yes.' Morgan's father nodded. 'To Florida. To Tampa, actually. And from there to Mango Key.'

Catherine stared at him. 'You're not serious!'

'Why not? If Morgan's not here, I'd lay odds he's with Steve Whitney. I'll know for sure tonight. When my agent calls.'

'But...' Catherine swallowed. 'I couldn't go there on my own.'

'Not on your own,' exclaimed the general. 'With me! Will you?'

Catherine was dazed. 'Why?'

'Because I think my son will be more pleased to see you than he will to see me.'

Catherine bent her head. 'I shouldn't bank on it.'

'Nevertheless, if he is there—will you?'

Catherine hesitated. All her common sense was telling her to turn him down, that seeing Morgan again, for whatever reason, was only going to make it that much harder in the end. He didn't want her. He had told her so. His father just needed someone else to lean on. Someone else to bear the brunt of his son's frustration.

But, in spite of all that, what she actually said was, 'Don't I need a visa?'

'Not any more.' General Lynch's face lit up. 'Does that mean you'll come?'

Catherine adjusted her spectacles with an unsteady hand. 'I have a job,' she said helplessly. 'I'd have to arrange to take some time off.'

'No problem. If Morgan is there—and I've told my agent *not* to contact him—we'll leave on Wednesday. Leave all the travel arrangements to me.'

Catherine shook her head. It didn't seem possible that she had actually agreed to travel more than three thousand miles with this man—a man she hadn't known until an hour ago! Provisionally agreed, a small voice added. It was always possible that Morgan wasn't there. And if he wasn't . . .

But she didn't want to think about that, and when General Lynch said, 'Shall we go?' she got up with alacrity.

'I'm afraid you've got a parking ticket,' she murmured, as they walked towards the Mercedes, but Morgan's father only grimaced.

'A small price to pay,' he remarked, opening her door. 'You've given me hope, Catherine. That's worth more than a million parking tickets!'

CHAPTER ELEVEN

HECTOR was especially affectionate when she got home, and Catherine wondered if he knew she was going to have to put him in a cattery for a few days. It would be his first experience of being boarded out, and, in spite of her eagerness to see Morgan again, she wasn't looking forward to leaving Hector with a stranger. But she had no alternative. She couldn't leave him to fend for himself. He was too valuable to her. She couldn't run the risk of someone kidnapping him.

Picking him up, she buried her face in his soft fur, and he purred approvingly. He hadn't had much attention these past weeks, and she felt guiltily aware of her neglect. 'I wish I could take you with me, but I can't,' she said, carrying him into the kitchen. 'I'm sure you wouldn't enjoy it anyway. This trip is strictly for the birds.'

She phoned Aunt Agnes at six o'clock, and told her what she was going to do. Her aunt took the news in her usual philosophical way, then she said shrewdly, 'And what will you do, afterwards? Come home again?'

Catherine's stomach hollowed. 'I don't know,' she admitted honestly. 'I suppose so.'

'And do you think you can cope with that?' Aunt Agnes's tone was gentle, but persistent.

'I'll have to, won't I?' replied her niece tightly. 'But I am going. If—if he is there, I have to see him again.'

'Very well.' Her aunt accepted her decision, without further comment. 'But what about Hector? What are you going to do with him?'

165

Catherine sighed. 'I'll have to find a cattery to take
him.' Then, remembering her aunt had cats, too, she
added, 'Do you know of a good one?'

'Yes. Here,' declared Aunt Agnes flatly. 'I'll look after
him while you're away. Don't worry, I won't let Castor
and Pollux hurt him. And at least you won't have to
spend your time worrying about him.'

'Oh—will you do that?' Catherine was so relieved,
she could have cried. 'I feel so bad about leaving him,
after the way I've treated him these last few weeks. I
was afraid that if I put him in a cattery, he'd pine.'

'Well, that's something you won't have to face,' said
her aunt briskly. 'I'll pick him up on Tuesday evening.
If there's any change in the arrangements, let me know.'

'I will. And thanks.'

'Good luck,' retorted her aunt drily, and rang off
before the conversation got too emotional.

On Monday, Catherine saw John Humphries, and arranged with him for her to take a few days' holiday. 'I
think I need a break,' she said, without elaborating, and
John, who had been aware of how hard she had been
driving herself these past weeks, made no demur.

'Take tomorrow, too,' he said, when she broached the
idea of starting her holiday on Wednesday. 'We can
manage. Just give what you're doing to Mel. He hasn't
been exactly overworked lately.'

General Lynch had said he would phone, as soon as
he had any news. Catherine had half expected him to
phone on Sunday evening, but he hadn't, and by Monday
evening she was getting anxious. He must know something, she thought. Why didn't he let her know? Even
if the news was negative—which she dreaded—she'd
rather know the worst.

Remembering the night she had put off taking her
bath, waiting for Morgan to call, she decided not to alter
her normal schedule. If the phone did ring, she could

easily jump out and run into the bedroom. And she wouldn't take very long.

In the event, she was drying herself when the doorbell rang. Frowning, she quickly catalogued all the possibilities, and then came to the unwilling conclusion that it must be her mother. The probability of its being General Lynch was simply too disruptive to consider. She didn't want to build her hopes up, just to have them dashed again when she discovered it was Mrs Lambert, come to find out why she hadn't seen her.

Wrapping her towelling bathrobe about her, she ran downstairs. In her present state of anticipation, the possibility that her visitor might not be friendly didn't occur to her, so that when she opened the door and Neil pushed past her without her permission, she was too shocked to stop him.

Her immobility didn't last long, however. Almost instantaneously, a sense of outrage gripped her, and without even bothering to lock the front door she charged after him into the living-room.

Hector, sensing a confrontation, was bristling on the hearthrug, but Catherine scarcely looked at him. Her attention was concentrated on her ex-husband, pacing aggressively back and forth across the floor.

'What the hell do you think you're doing?' she demanded, her spectacles sliding down her damp nose as she spoke. 'This is *my* house, Neil. You have no right to barge in here as if——'

'Shut up!' Neil's temper was explosive, and, while he had never been violent, he could be objectionable, as she well knew. 'What did you expect me to do? Ignore it?'

'Ignore what?' Catherine clenched her fists. 'Neil——'

'When you said there was someone else, I didn't like it. You know that. But I never thought even you would sink that low!'

Catherine blinked. What was he talking about? He knew nothing about Morgan, and there was no one else. Unless he had seen Denzil. It occurred to her that it might amuse Denzil to tell Neil about Morgan. Particularly if he thought it would hurt her.

'Neil—I think you'd better go——'

'Not yet.' He halted then, and swung round on her. 'How does it feel to have an old man crawling all over you?' he demanded contemptuously. 'Is he any good at it? Better than you, I'll bet.'

Catherine clutched the lapels of her bathrobe. 'I—don't know what you're talking about,' she protested. But she did. Somehow, Neil must have seen her with Morgan's father. He thought General Lynch was the man she had been dating!

'Don't give me that!' Neil was incensed, so incensed that Catherine suspected he had called at a pub for some Dutch courage before coming here. He couldn't have been home. What excuse would he have given Marie for going out again so soon? 'I saw you with him,' he snarled, gazing at her with glittering eyes. 'Going into Lowrey's together. You didn't see me, did you? Oh, no! You were too intent on letting him maul you!'

Catherine sighed. 'You're wrong——'

'I'm not wrong. I saw you, I tell you. You're not exactly unnoticeable, Cat. Thinner, perhaps, but just as long-legged!'

'I mean, it wasn't what you thought,' said Catherine wearily, and then, realising she didn't have to explain herself to him, she caught herself up. 'I'd like you to go. Now! I don't wish to discuss this.'

'I'll bet you don't.' Neil moved forward, and, although Catherine moved aside to let him pass, he didn't go. Instead, he came closer, looking down into the V of her bathrobe with insolent, probing eyes. 'You didn't think I'd see you, did you?' he sneered. 'Well, we often have lunch at Lowrey's on Sunday, and we had just got into our car when the big Mercedes pulled up. I might not have noticed you, even then, if you hadn't parked in a no-parking zone.' His lips twisted. 'Who is he, Cat? Some old guy with pots of money, I suppose. God, couldn't you do any better than that?'

Catherine slapped him then, her fingers stinging where they made contact with his cheek. How dared he? she thought. *How dared he?* What she did was her affair, and no one else's. How dare he come here and behave like some latter-day Karenin?

Her emotions were so incensed that she didn't stop to think that Neil's emotions might be equally as high. She had never struck him before, it was true; but then, he had never been so objectionable before. No doubt he had had no reason to be, she acknowledged. She had been the innocent party in their divorce. He had been the one playing fast and loose with their relationship. But now it was different. Now, he was getting a taste of what it was like to be powerless to stop what was happening. Not that he had any right to those feelings, she argued. Neil had forfeited any right to a say in her affairs when he'd gone to live with Marie.

Nevertheless, as he lunged for her, she realised that what should be, and what *was*, were two entirely different things. For some reason, Neil had decided that the rules no longer applied, and she felt the first twinge of alarm when he grabbed her arm.

Even then, she had no inkling of his ultimate objective. In her heart of hearts, she didn't really believe Neil would hurt her, but when he twisted her arm behind her back, and jerked her towards him, alarm gave way to real fear.

'*Neil!*' she protested, not finding it as easy as she had thought to escape him now. He was hurting her arm, and every time she tried to pull away he gave it another vicious twist. 'Neil, this is ridiculous——'

'How does it feel to be at my mercy for a change?' he demanded. 'You were always in control, before, weren't you? Or at least you thought you were. High and mighty Catherine, with her clever degree, and her clever job! Always thinking she was better than us lesser mortals——'

'That's not true!'

Catherine was horrified, and even Hector had come to press himself against her legs, as if trying in his own feline way to give her his support.

'It is true,' snorted Neil, and, looking into his contorted face, Catherine realised he was completely out of control. And she was frightened. In all the time they had lived together, he had never behaved like this, and she wondered what had happened to drive him over the edge. She couldn't believe it was seeing her with General Lynch. It wasn't as if they had behaved like lovers. There had to be something else.

'Let me go, Neil,' she said, struggling desperately to keep the note of panic out of her voice. Somehow she had to talk him out of this, and fighting with him was not going to do it. 'Can't we sit down, and talk about this like normal people——?'

'Normal people?' he grunted. 'You're not normal. A normal woman would have given me a family! Instead of which, your job was always more important than what I wanted.'

'Neil, you know it wasn't my job that stopped us from having children——'

'You women; you're all the same,' he overrode her harshly. 'I really thought when I married Marie that she'd be different. But she's not. She's just like you. What I want just doesn't count.'

Catherine blinked. Was that what this was all about? The fact that Marie had refused to have a baby? It sounded crazy, but it was the only alternative she had.

'Listen, Neil,' she said, wincing as he pressed her arm to the limit of its endurance. 'You—you and Marie have only been together two years. Give her time. She's young. You're still young yourself. You've got years ahead——'

'What would you know about Marie and me?' he retorted. 'You with your designer job, and your designer home, and your designer cat——'

He kicked out at Hector then, and the cat's yowl of protest gave Catherine the determination she needed to bring up her knee and drive it into Neil's groin. His howl of anguish drowned out the cat's but, although Catherine managed to free her arm from his grasp, she stumbled over Hector as she tried to get away. She fell, her spectacles flying, and her head grazing the hearth as she did so. And, as she lay there in a dazed haze, Neil flung himself on top of her.

'You bitch!' he grated. 'Don't you think you can try those alley cat tactics on me, and get away with it. I've been bloody polite and civilised so far, but now I'm going to teach you——'

'Why don't you teach me instead?'

Even in her state of drifting consciousness, Catherine recognised that voice. Although her mind was swimming, she would have recognised Morgan's voice anywhere, and, although she was sure she must be hallucinating, it gave her the strength to hold on to her reason.

'I'm neither polite, nor civilised,' that pleasant drawl continued smoothly. 'Much more of a challenge, wouldn't you say?'

Neil moved then, swinging round on his knees to face the speaker, and Catherine struggled up on to one elbow to see Morgan himself propped casually against the living-room door.

But Morgan wasn't looking at her. His attention was all on the man who was now scrambling rather inelegantly to his feet, and, even as she watched, he came forward and grasped a handful of Neil's shirt front.

There was a look of such murderous hatred in Morgan's face at that moment that Catherine briefly feared for Neil's safety. Morgan was so much bigger than he was, and infinitely stronger. Not to mention having the kind of experience of fighting that Neil could only guess at.

But even as her ex-husband started to bluster that Morgan was interfering in something he knew nothing about, Morgan turned his head and looked at her. The look in his eyes was no longer frightening; it was hot and possessive, though, when he saw the smear of blood on her temple, the hand that wasn't gripping Neil's shirt clenched aggressively.

Ignoring Neil's frantic attempts to explain himself, he brought his arm back and telegraphed a powerful fist into the other man's face, and Neil collapsed like a house of cards. Then, hauling him up again, Morgan hustled him out of the door, and presently Catherine heard the front door slam.

Seconds later, Morgan was back, striding across the floor, and dropping down on to his knees beside her. 'Are you all right?' he demanded, examining the slight gash on her temple with almost professional detachment. But he wasn't detached. Catherine had only to look into his eyes to see that. 'He didn't hurt you?'

'O—only my pride,' she breathed unsteadily, and his eyes darkened.

'Who was he? Why did you let him in?'

'Neil,' whispered Catherine. 'Just Neil.'

'Your ex-husband?'

'Mmm.' She tried to clear her throat. 'Who—who did you think it was?'

'I didn't know what to think,' he muttered, and then, as if the need to touch her overrode his desire to assure himself that she was indeed unharmed, he pulled her up into his arms.

The mouth that covered hers was hard and passionate, his fingers at the back of her head strong and possessive, but she realised he was shaking. As she lifted her hand to clutch his neck, she could feel the tremors running over his taut body, and, although her head was aching, the need to reassure him was the only thing that mattered to her.

Wrapping her arms around his neck, she pulled him down to her, and his weight almost drove all the breath from her lungs. But she didn't care. It was so good to feel his arms around her again, and when his tongue plunged into her mouth she matched his sensuous exploration with an exploration of her own.

'I love you,' she breathed, not caring that she was exposing herself to rejection or worse, and his arms tightened about her.

She had wanted him so much, she thought dazedly, as he parted the lapels of her robe to expose her warm breasts to his hungry mouth. She didn't know how he was here, and she didn't care. She only knew that whatever he wanted from her, she would give it. And gladly.

He was wearing a tweed jacket, and, needing to get closer to him, Catherine pushed the jacket off his shoulders, and Morgan shrugged out of it. Underneath, the rough cotton of his shirt was abrasive to her hands, but she could feel the heat of his skin through it, and smell the male scent of his body. And he smelt so good, she thought, her fingers invading the neckline of his shirt. So good!

Her bathrobe was open now, her slim body exposed to his possessive hands. He caressed her urgently, looking down at her as he did so, his expression taut, but sensual. Catherine felt no sense of embarrassment beneath his intent gaze. Indeed, just knowing it was Morgan who

was looking at her in that oddly wondering way made
her whole body weak with longing.

'You're—so—beautiful,' he groaned, bending his head
to brush his lips to the dark curls that sheltered her
womanhood, and her legs parted almost involuntarily.

His fingers slid between her legs, and then, with an
anguished groan, his hands went to the belt of his jeans.
Supporting his weight on one arm, he dragged the jeans
and the silk underpants beneath them down to his knees,
and Catherine, almost afraid to look at what he was
doing, stared up into his dark, sweating face.

'God! *God!*' he groaned, almost like a litany, and
Catherine closed her eyes so she didn't have to see his
raw frustration. If only there was some way she could
help him, she thought, tears stinging her cheeks. If only
there were something she could do!

And then, incredibly, she felt the hard proof of his
manhood, hot between her legs. As her eyes darted open,
he guided himself into her, and the sensation it created
was liquid fire.

'Oh, God,' he said, against her mouth, and with a
little cry she wound her arms and legs about him.

It was over fairly quickly, but Catherine didn't care.
Morgan had made love to her, and the shudders that
shook his body long after he had slumped across her
were proof of his satisfaction. Not that she needed any
proof, Catherine thought triumphantly. She had felt the
drenching spill of his seed inside her, and never had she
experienced such a shattering sensation as that.

It was some minutes before Morgan was able to push
himself up from her, and when he did his eyes were raw
with emotion. With trembling fingers, he smoothed her
damp hair back from her forehead, and then, with the
utmost tenderness, he kissed her.

'I love you,' he said simply, releasing her mouth to
rest his forehead against hers. 'And now you know how
much.'

Catherine cried then, the tension of the last hour translating itself into a hiccupping storm of weeping, and, with a gentle touch, Morgan licked the tears from her cheeks.

'I know,' he said huskily. 'Believe me, I know. But— God help me! It's over now.'

Catherine nodded, not trusting herself to speak, and, after divesting himself of his boots and trousers, and the shirt, which she had already unbuttoned, Morgan gathered her into his arms and got to his feet.

'Let's go to bed,' he said, and she thought those words had never sounded so good.

Catherine awakened next morning, to find Hector staring at her in cool disdain from the open bedroom doorway. It was obvious he was not pleased, and, remembering how Neil had kicked him the night before, she felt a momentary sense of regret. But only a momentary one. Without Hector's intervention, she might never have tried to escape Neil, might never have fallen and nearly brained herself, might never have frightened Morgan into——

Her thoughts broke off at that point, as the realisation of the meaning of the warm body curled, spoon-like, around hers brought its own delicious awareness. Morgan was still asleep, his arm beneath her head, his face buried in her hair, and, remembering how they had spent the last twelve hours, she couldn't honestly blame him. He must be exhausted, she thought, stretching with a delightful sense of lethargy. She was pretty exhausted herself. But so happy that she wanted to explode.

Realising it was daylight beyond the drawn curtains, she squinted at the clock on the table beside the bed. It was after ten o'clock, she saw, with some amazement. No wonder Hector was giving her the evil eye. He wanted to be fed.

Reluctantly, she eased herself away from Morgan, but she hadn't reached the edge of the bed before he came after her. 'Where're you going?' he protested, stopping her by the simple procedure of sliding a possessive arm and leg across her body, and, feeling the unmistakeable pressure of his arousal against her thigh, her resolution deserted her.

'Hector needs feeding,' she said, but there was little conviction in the words, and Morgan's mouth took on a sensual curve.

'So do I,' he said huskily, rolling on to his back and pulling her on top of him. 'Do you still love me?'

'Madly,' she breathed, only half in fun, and then, as his eyes darkened, she lowered her head and covered his mouth with hers.

His response was instantaneous, and, presently, he rolled her over again, and parting her legs, eased his way into her. The throbbing ache that seemed to know only a temporary satiation was satisfied again, and Catherine thought how amazing it was that she had lived all these years without ever understanding what she had been missing. Neil had never made her feel even a half of what Morgan made her feel, and she realised now how wonderful love could be.

'I can't get enough of you,' he muttered, inadvertently voicing what she had been thinking, and she opened her mouth against his chest.

'Me, too,' she breathed, as filaments of hair invaded her nose and mouth. 'Oh, Morgan, I'm so glad you came back.'

'So am I,' he agreed fervently, rolling on to his side, facing her, one leg draped possessively around her. 'If that—creep—had touched you, I'd have killed him!'

She thought he would, too. There had been such an expression of hatred in his face when he had seen what Neil was trying to do to her. But he had controlled it, she remembered with some pride. Apart from ex-

punging that one chunk of frustration, he had acted with
extreme restraint, and any fears she had had that his
years in Vietnam might have eroded his self-control had
been dispelled.

'How did you get here anyway?' she exclaimed. 'Was
it—your father?'

She hated asking him that. She hated the thought that
he might only be here because General Lynch had asked
him to come.

'My father!' Morgan's mouth twisted. 'Did you know
he'd sent his pet intelligence agent looking for me? Oh,
yes. Of course, you did. He told you, didn't he?'

Catherine swallowed. 'Yes.' She hesitated. 'Did—did
he find you?'

'Who? Dwight?' Morgan stroked a teasing finger
down her breast, enjoying the way her nipple hardened
instantly. 'How could he? He didn't know where I was.'

'But...' Catherine caught her breath as he took her
nipple between his thumb and forefinger, and gently
tugged. 'I—thought—your father thought you were in
Florida.'

'I know.' Morgan looked at her through narrowed
eyes, watching her helpless arousal. 'But I wasn't.'

Catherine removed his hand from her breast. 'Please,'
she said, appealingly, 'I want to know what happened.'

'All right.' Realising he couldn't go on holding her
and relate what had happened, Morgan turned on to his
back. But he turned his head towards her. 'I did go to
the States,' he admitted softly. 'A few days after—well,
a few days after you'd come to the apartment, I realised
I couldn't go on living in the same town and not see you.
I knew it was only a matter of time before I'd come
looking for you again, and I thought that wasn't fair—
to either of us.'

'Oh, Morgan!'

'Well. You knew how I felt,' he reminded her. 'That
was why I knew I had to get away. I told myself I needed

some time to myself; time to think about the future, and what I was going to do with my life. But the truth was, I was fighting the need to throw myself on your mercy, and let the future take care of itself.'

'Oh, love!'

She leaned over and kissed him then, and it was with the utmost reluctance that he let her go again.

'I thought—if I went back home—I might see things in their real perspective,' he continued huskily.

Catherine frowned. 'But—your father said he hadn't seen you.'

'He hadn't.' Morgan grimaced. 'I didn't go see him. I knew if I did, I'd have to explain what I was doing there, when I was supposed to be working at the Embassy, and I couldn't face that.'

'But—he does care about you.'

'Oh, I know that.' Morgan sighed. 'I've been a great disappointment to the old man, and if he hadn't cared about me I guess he'd have washed his hands of me by now.'

'That's not true.' Catherine propped herself up on one elbow and looked down at him. 'He's very proud of you. He said so. He blames himself for your—estrangement. I just don't think he knows how to tell you.'

Morgan absorbed this, and then shook his head. 'Well—maybe,' he conceded wryly. 'But nothing can alter the fact that I'm not the son he would have chosen for himself.'

Catherine hesitated. 'So—where did you go?'

'Oh . . .' With his eyes on her mouth, Morgan had to concentrate to remember what he had been saying. 'Well, I visited a few of the places that had meant something to me in the past. Los Angeles; I wanted to go to university there, but I guess the old man told you what happened.' And at her nod, he went on, 'I went to Arlington. Not to the house, but to the cemetery. My mother's buried there. Not in the military cemetery, of course, although I visited it, too.' His eyes darkened briefly. 'Some guys I knew are buried there.'

Catherine bent her head. She could imagine how painful that must have been for him.

'Anyway,' he said, more positively, 'last of all, I went to a place called Lawton Heights. It's in the Catskill Mountains; they're in New York State. There's a clinic there I once knew very well. I should do. I spent two years there.'

Catherine inclined her head. 'And?'

'I talked to the doctor who had treated me. I told him—I had met someone, and—that I loved her, and wanted to marry her.'

'Oh, Morgan.'

'He examined me. He said I was in good shape.' Morgan gave a rueful laugh at this point. 'Of course, I didn't believe him. But at least it convinced me I wasn't going out of my head.' He hesitated. 'He also said there was no reason why I should remain——'

He broke off, and Catherine buried her face in the hollow of his neck. She knew how hard it must be for him to tell her these things, but she also wanted him to know how much it meant to her.

'That was when I knew I had to come back to England,' he said. 'Weak, eh?' He shook his head. 'Whatever, I couldn't live without you.'

Catherine hugged him closer. 'You won't have to.'

'No?' Morgan's dark expression softened. 'Does that mean you'll have me?'

'Try and get away,' muttered Catherine, winding herself about him, and for a while there was a satisfying silence in the bedroom.

CHAPTER TWELVE

'AT LEAST I won't need to take sleeping tablets any more,' Morgan teased her an hour later, as they shared a belated breakfast in the kitchen. 'I'm shattered! I've never made love in a bath before.'

Catherine dimpled, only a slight trace of colour appearing beneath the rims of her spectacles. 'I didn't hear you complaining,' she murmured, as Hector offered a satisfied growl at being fed at last.

'I'm not.' In her peach towelling bathrobe, Morgan was disarmingly sensual. 'I'm just making an observation. Do you want to come here, and I'll prove it?'

'I've got to get dressed,' protested Catherine, but she let him pull her on to his knee, her silk kimono parting provocatively to reveal a long, curvaceous thigh. 'Didn't you say your father was expecting us at the apartment in half an hour?'

'Mmm.' Morgan nuzzled her shoulder. 'But he can wait. I told him not to hold his breath.'

Catherine gurgled with laughter. Morgan had told her he had been as surprised to find his father at his apartment, the day before, as General Lynch had been to see him. But prolonged explanations had had to wait, after his father had confessed what he and Catherine had been planning to do. Instead, Morgan had come straight round to her house, to tell her he was back. And she knew the rest.

However, this morning Morgan had stirred himself sufficiently to phone his father, and let the old man know that, contrary to his fears, his son was no longer a victim of his experiences. Catherine could guess how General

Lynch must feel, but, even as she considered his delight, a painful realisation struck her.

Pushing herself off Morgan's knee, she went to stand at the window, looking out at the bare winter garden. She was like the garden, she thought: barren, and unproductive. With her for a daughter-in-law, General Lynch would never have the grandson he so obviously would want.

'What's the matter?'

Ever perceptive of Catherine's feelings, Morgan had come to stand behind her, sliding his arms around her waist and across her stomach, pressing her back against his lean, strong body. Catherine allowed herself the luxury of resting against him for a long, languorous minute, and then she determinedly tried to pull away again.

'I am,' she said, with difficulty. 'Have—have you forgotten? I—can't give you any children.'

'I hadn't forgotten,' declared Morgan huskily. 'So? What does it matter? We have each other. Isn't that enough?'

Catherine twisted round in his arms, and took his face between her palms. 'It is for me,' she said painfully. 'But you—you deserve someone who—who can give you sons and daughters, as beautiful as you are yourself.'

Morgan shook his head. 'I deserve you,' he told her firmly. 'I've convinced myself of that. Don't tell me you're going to take it away from me now.'

'Oh, Morgan!' She slipped her arms around his neck. 'I love you so much.'

'Do you?' Morgan's smile was teasing. 'I think I'm going to need a lot more proof of that.'

When Mrs Lambert arrived about three-quarters of an hour later, they were still not dressed, and when Catherine answered the door in her kimono her mother looked at her askance.

'Good heavens!' she exclaimed, when Catherine stepped back to let her into the house. 'When Agnes told me what you were doing, I didn't believe her.'

Catherine's eyes widened, and she glanced revealingly up the stairs, before leading her mother into the kitchen. 'Er—what did Aunt Agnes tell you?'

'Not a lot,' her mother replied shortly, her sharp eyes noting the two sets of breakfast dishes still occupying the table. 'What's going on, Catherine? Don't I have a right to know?'

'Of course you do.' Catherine caught her lower lip between her teeth. 'As a matter of fact, you're going to be the first to know: I'm getting married again.'

'*Married!*' Mrs Lambert was clearly stunned. 'But Agnes didn't say anything about you getting married. She just gave me some garbled story about her looking after Hector, while you went off to the United States with some old man, who was searching for his son.' She broke off. 'You're not—marrying that old man, are you, Catherine?'

'Judge for yourself,' remarked Morgan, who had come down the stairs, and along the hall while they were speaking. He had rescued his clothes earlier, and, although the stubble of a night's growth of beard darkened his jawline, he still looked devastatingly attractive.

Mrs Lambert turned confusedly to face him, her eyes showing her astonishment when she realised that the man standing behind her was one of the most attractive men she had ever seen. Not only that, he was a man in the prime of his life.

'But, you're not—you can't be——' she began, and Catherine, who had never known her mother at a loss for words, exchanged a humorous look with Morgan.

'No,' he said, smiling as he came forward to offer her his hand. 'That was my father. How do you do, Mrs Lambert? I'm Morgan Lynch.'

Catherine's mother gulped as her hand was swallowed up in his much larger one, and she turned to look at her daughter again with bewildered eyes. 'I—don't understand any of this,' she told her, not without some vexation. 'Catherine, why didn't you tell me?'

'It's a long story,' declared Morgan disarmingly, drawing out a chair from the table, and pressing her mother into it. 'Cat and I have known one another for some time, but it's only recently that we've realised we can't live without each other. It's as simple as that. And, as Cat says, you are the first to know we're getting married. Even my father doesn't know that yet.'

Mrs Lambert shook her head, as Morgan went to slip a possessive arm about her daughter's waist. For so long, she had hoped that Catherine might find happiness with someone else, but never in her wildest dreams had she imagined that her quiet, bespectacled daughter would find someone like Morgan Lynch. And yet, watching them together, she had no doubts about the depth of their feelings for one another. The way they looked at one another, the way they touched—she almost felt as if she was intruding. But they were both looking at her with such obvious happiness in their faces that she quickly abandoned any thought of leaving. Besides, there was a wedding to arrange, she thought smugly. And that was one occasion Agnes wouldn't pre-empt.

Three months later, Catherine came out on to the balcony of the single-storeyed villa Morgan had bought for them on Mango Key, to find her husband reclining lazily on a striped, cushioned lounger. In dark sunglasses, and swimming shorts that were only barely decent, he looked fit, and tanned, and outrageously handsome, not at all perturbed by the heat or the humidity. That was one thing he had told her about his days in Vietnam: the fact that he, and his fellow prisoners, had had to get used to all extremes of temperature. He seldom felt the cold, but equally he seemed indifferent to the heat. But at least he no longer had those nightmares, she thought with satisfaction. He hadn't told her everything yet. But he would. Slowly but surely, his mind was healing, too.

Hector was with him, stretched out on the tiles, watching with a jaundiced eye the nervous tactics of a humming bird. The bird was trying to hover over the pink blossoms of the bougainvillaea, that grew in such profusion over the balcony, while keeping an eye on the cat at the same time. If it only knew, Hector considered hunting for his food far too energetic in this heat, Catherine thought wryly. Besides, with the waters of the gulf giving up a veritable banquet of fish, he had only to wait to be handed the juiciest morsels.

Hearing her footsteps, both males turned their heads, but it was Morgan who came up off the lounger, and came to meet her. 'Hey,' he said softly, turning up her face for his kiss. 'I missed you. What did he say?'

Catherine wondered how to tell him. So much had happened since they became a couple that it wasn't difficult to understand how she had overlooked it. First, there had been seeing Morgan's father, and getting his blessing, and then all the excitement of the wedding. It had just been a family affair, with Morgan's sisters and their families flying over from New England, and her mother and Aunt Agnes, vying with each other in their choice of dress. Morgan's sisters had been nice, welcoming her into the family with real affection, proving, if any proof were needed, that Morgan's happiness was all they cared about.

Morgan's father had surprised them all, too. When Morgan had mentioned going back to the Embassy in London, General Lynch had declared that in his opinion it would be better if his son made his home in the United States. 'I'm an old man,' he said. 'I can't fly to London every time I want to see you. Mrs Lambert, now, she's just a slip of a girl. Crossing the Atlantic won't prove too arduous for her.'

Of course, Catherine's mother had fallen for that, hook, line and sinker. Or perhaps she had only pretended to, Catherine thought now. Whatever, she had made no demur when her daughter and new son-in-law had accepted Morgan's father's suggestion. As Catherine knew, her mother had her own life to lead, and she had always enjoyed travelling.

But the biggest surprise of all had been when General Lynch had disclosed the news that he owned the controlling interest in a condominium complex on Mango Key. As well as the apartments, there was a golf club, and marina, and, if Morgan was prepared to do it, he could go down there and manage the place for him.

Of course, Catherine knew why he had done it, but that didn't stop her from giving him a particularly enthusiastic hug when she heard the news. The general was learning, she thought, guessing it would still be some time before he and Morgan became close friends. But they loved one another and that was what really mattered. Catherine believed in love.

Now, she dropped her clutch bag on to the drinks trolley, and smoothed her palms down the skirt of her loose dress. She had worn the hot pink dress with its flattering spaghetti straps deliberately, because it was light and cool, and it was one of Morgan's favourites. But now, she wondered if subconsciously she had known the real reason why she was wearing it. It was so apt, and her heart, which had been pounding ever since the doctor had delivered his ultimatum, skipped a couple of beats.

'He said—I'm pregnant,' she said with a rush, unable when it came down to it, to spin the news out. 'I—I said it wasn't possible, but he said it definitely was.'

Morgan's hands gripped her shoulders very tightly. 'You mean——?'

'I mean, my throwing up every morning has a perfectly innocent explanation,' said Catherine lightly, anxious that he should be as pleased about the news as she was. 'Are—are you pleased? I couldn't believe it when he told me.'

Morgan pulled her into his arms, burying his face in the hollow of her neck. 'Of course I'm pleased,' he muttered roughly. 'But are you? It's not something you expected, is it?'

Catherine caught her breath. 'Oh, love,' she whispered, turning her lips against his shoulder, 'to be having *your* baby! Are you joking? If I couldn't believe it, it's because I wanted it so much.'

He kissed her then, his mouth warm and passionate, sharing with her the very special delight of their love. Her spectacles, which always got in the way in moments like this, were quickly discarded on to the trolley beside her bag, and, picking her up in his arms, he carried her back to the sun lounger.

'So, where did you get the idea that you couldn't have children?' Morgan demanded, a few minutes later, and Catherine, whose hand had been straying innocently to the waistband of his shorts, gave a rueful sigh.

'I don't know,' she said. 'Or, at least, I do.' She looked up at him with a grimace. 'Neil told me.'

Morgan's eyes darkened. 'And what gave him the right to make judgements of that sort?' he asked harshly. 'I knew I should have flattened that guy when I had the chance.'

'You did,' said Catherine, with a guilty giggle, but Morgan shook his head.

'Not nearly,' he told her, loosening the strap of her dress on her right shoulder. 'Go on. I'm listening. What medical qualifications does he have?'

'None.' Catherine felt her cheeks turning pink. 'He went to one of those clinics, where they make tests; that

sort of thing. His result came back positive. I saw it.'
She lifted her shoulders. 'He said it had to be me.'

Morgan shook his head. 'It didn't occur to you that
you just might not have been compatible, did it? I mean,
let's face it, he and his second wife don't have any kids,
do they?'

'No.' Catherine's eyes widened. 'Do you think that's
why he made all those accusations about her?' She had
told Morgan everything that had happened between her
and Neil, including the unsatisfactory relationship they
had had when they were married.

'Probably,' agreed Morgan now. 'Though my guess
is he'd realised he'd made a mistake. He wanted you
back, baby. But he was too late.'

'He was always too late,' said Catherine, touching his
cheek. 'As soon as I met you, I knew what Neil and I
had had...' She shook her head. 'Well, you know.'

'Tell me,' said Morgan wickedly, and Catherine did
so shyly, pressing her lips against his ear.

'What about your job?' Morgan asked at last, playing
with the other strap of her sun-dress. 'I know you said
you were going to free-lance, but——'

'I don't care about my job.' Catherine gazed at him
adoringly. 'I'm going to have a baby! Our baby. I'll think
about my job when I've got nothing better to do.'

Morgan shifted then, until she was lying on the
lounger, and he was supporting himself over her. 'I guess
this means we'll have to—well, be a little less energetic
in our relationship, hmm?'

'Don't you believe it!' Catherine grasped his neck with
possessive hands, and pulled him down on top of her.
'The doctor says I'm already three months into my term.
And you know what that means, don't you?'

'You conceived the first time we made love?' suggested Morgan, his voice just a little thick. 'What a way
to start our lives together.' He grinned. 'Though, in the
circumstances, I can't say I'm really surprised.'

'That wasn't what I meant,' declared Catherine, sliding her hands beneath the waistband of his shorts, and inching them over his hips. 'I meant—everyone knows, you only have to take care for the first three months, in a normal pregnancy. And as the doctor says I'm excessively normal, and we didn't even know——'

'I guess we don't have to worry, right?' Morgan finished for her lazily. 'Hey, I hope you locked that door when you came in. I wouldn't want Steve to be embarrassed.'

'Would you be?' asked Catherine, as the second strap of her dress came undone, and Morgan laughed.

'Me? I'm used to an audience,' he said, with an endearing lack of self-consciousness, and Catherine thought Hector turned his head the other way.